I0616912

Sandpipers

SANDPIPERS' SECRETS

JADE ARCHER

SANDPIPERS' SECRETS

Dedication

For Charles — because your friendship, help and
support mean so much to me.

Chapter One

Brody took a deep breath and ran his hands down his carefully pressed dress pants one more time. It was the best he could do for the moment, he decided nervously. Surely, no one would knock him back for an interview just because the creases in his trousers were a bit crooked or his shirt cuffs and collar were looking a little worse for wear. He certainly hoped not anyway. He had to get a job, and soon. He just had to.

He pulled his wallet out and rummaged through it again. Unfortunately, there wasn't any more in there now than there had been an hour ago, or the hour before that, or when he had arrived home from job hunting last night.

Looks like I'm walking from now on. Brody sighed and ran his hand through his hair. Or at least until I get hold of a paycheque.

Pushing his wallet back into his pocket and readjusting his pants around his thin waist, Brody began to pray the weather held out.

Just long enough to get a job and get back on track, he begged, with very little hope that anyone would be answering his pleas—either on the weather or the job seeking front. No one had ever given him an inch before. He'd had to earn each and every lucky break he'd ever come across. Usually the hard way. He didn't see why things should be any different now just because he and his brother Wolf had moved halfway across the country—Illinois to California in one long, harrowing road trip of hitching, hiking and flat out begging for rides.

But it had been a good move. The only move they could make really if they wanted to pull themselves out of the hole they'd been born into. Being in a strange place, not knowing anyone, with no job and nearly no money...*that* wasn't so good. And Wolf...well as much as he loved Wolf, he couldn't deny that his brother definitely complicated matters.

Glancing up, Brody took the time to scrutinise his face in the bathroom mirror. Thick dark blond hair—slightly longer than it should be for job hunting because he couldn't afford a decent haircut—fell over pale blue eyes shadowed with worry. And there was every reason to be concerned. Things were getting pretty desperate when you couldn't even afford bus fare into the city.

He'd have to try looking for a job somewhere in the local area, he realised. Perhaps the little row of restaurants and cafés down by the pier would have something. Anything would do. Even casual work would be better than what he had at the moment—absolutely nothing. And it wouldn't be the first time he'd worked as a dish pig.

At the mere thought, sweat broke out across his brow and he felt his chest tighten with anxiety.

Working in a kitchen always reminded him of his first job, the one he'd picked up right after one of his mom's deadbeat boyfriends had kicked him out at fourteen. And hadn't it been a glorious start to his working life.

Shit! Just thinking about it made him sick to his stomach. Leonard. What a complete and utter bastard. He'd been the owner of the little grease pit Brody had finally managed to scrounge up work in. He'd also reasoned that because Brody had been desperate enough to work the low paid, loathsome job, he'd be willing to do other, loathsome things as well. The fat, pompous prick.

Of course, what happened next was my own stupid fault, Brody acknowledged grimly.

He'd been so naïve. He couldn't believe now that he had actually gone to the cops. It had been one of the biggest mistakes of his life. Because instead of arresting his boss, the police had listened to Leonard's bullshit story—and ended up charging Brody with soliciting and assault.

Brody still wasn't exactly sure how it had all transpired. Maybe Leonard had friends on the force or something. But regardless of how it happened, there ended up being just one short court appearance between Brody and his first stay in a juvenile detention centre.

Brody snorted and glanced away from the mirror. A hollow pain started up in his chest. He'd certainly learned some 'tricks' there.

Fuck! Now was not the time to be thinking about that shithead. Or the shithole juvie centre he'd ended up in. Or the numerous crappy foster care homes he'd continually run away from after that.

Grabbing the towel still draped over the sink where he had thrown it after his shower, Brody dabbed at his forehead and firmly pushed the memories away. Leaning forward against the cold, chipped porcelain bowl, he took several deep, calming breaths.

That was a long time ago now, he reminded himself. Nearly eight years. And over the last four years he had completely turned his life around.

You can't afford to get your clothes all messed up either, he reprimanded his reflection, brushing away at the water stain the edge of the sink had left behind when he'd leaned against it. These pants were the only ones he had that were clean and had any hope of getting him a foot in the door to snag an interview with a perspective employer. He straightened up and squared his shoulders.

Keep it together, Brod, he cautioned the slightly haggard looking boy looking back at him, well aware of how much depended on getting a job. And soon.

After carefully hanging the towel over the drying rack, he picked up his shoes and quietly headed for the kitchenette.

When he and Wolf had first arrived in the city about three weeks ago, they'd managed to rent a cheap, one-bedroom apartment in an older neighbourhood. The place looked like it had once been a single dwelling, but had since been split into two, smaller units.

At least they were relatively clean. Nowhere near as bad as some of the places he'd stayed in. The real bonus, however, was currently banging and clattering around in the tiny kitchen alcove.

Mrs. Tolimay, the little old lady who rented the unit next door.

Within twenty-four hours of moving in, the connecting door had been permanently wedged open and Mrs. Tolimay had all but adopted them. She was such a sweet, if somewhat forgetful old thing, and Brody couldn't begin to imagine what it would have been like if she weren't around now. In only three weeks she had become a permanent, wrinkled fixture in their lives.

Brody smiled as he recalled their first meeting. Or rather standing by while Mrs. Tolimay fussed over him and his brother—struggling to remember their names and crooning repeatedly about how cute the two of them were. He suspected they reminded her of some long lost relatives or other somewhere along the line. Perhaps grandchildren. Or even great-grandchildren.

As he cautiously stepped through the archway into the kitchen, Brody paused for a moment to watch her fondly. She was short, barely reaching his shoulder, and round and plump like he had always imagined a good granny should be—not that Brody had any personal experience on that front. He found her vague smile and faint scent of roses…comforting. He wished he'd had someone like her in his life when he was growing up. Maybe things would have turned out a whole lot different if he had.

Shaking his head at himself, he pushed the thoughts away to the 'get-the-fuck-over-it' file of regrets and disappointments in his head. At the end of the day, he was just thankful she was here now. Thinking about the harsh realities of his childhood wouldn't do anybody any good.

He knocked politely on the wall, so as not to barge in and frighten her. "Mrs. Tolimay, I'm off now."

Brody could see she was looking a little more lost than usual and frowned in concern. He really didn't like the idea of leaving her when she was like this, but he didn't have much choice. At the moment, she was the only sane person he knew in this strange new city. Well, sane might be a bit of an exaggeration, but at least she wasn't an axe-wielding, bat-shit crazy maniac. He'd known a few of those in his time, too.

Mrs. Tolimay waved absently as she muttered to herself and started pulling out the last few tins Brody had in reserve in the pantry cupboard. He shook his head in resignation. Hopefully, she wouldn't have the place pulled apart before he got back. Oh well. There was really nothing he could do about it if she did. He had to go out to find work, or they wouldn't have a place for her to pull apart come the next rent day.

He turned away and carefully crept back down the hallway, shoes still in hand. As he passed the bedroom door, he eyed it warily. He knew he should probably go in and check on Wolf before he left, but he really didn't want to wake his brother up. He'd been sick for a couple of days now and had been in a spectacularly foul mood as a result.

Hesitating for several moments, Brody eventually decided just to go without looking in. Hopefully, Wolf would stay asleep and wouldn't give poor Mrs. Tolimay any trouble.

After making his way out the front door, he double-checked it was securely locked and bolted behind him. You couldn't be too careful in a new place. He wasn't sure what the neighbourhood was really like because he hadn't had a proper chance to scout it out, what with the move and desperate job hunting and Wolf getting sick. But since it was about the cheapest place he could find for rent at the time, he assumed it wasn't without its problems.

One day, he promised, they'd live somewhere nice. And they wouldn't have to worry about where next week's rent was coming from. Or whether someone was going to try and steal it before they could hand it over.

* * * *

"Come on, Zak," Lark whined. "You promised we could go for a picnic today. Rio's even opening up the restaurant for us so we can have a few extra hours."

"Extra hours to sleep," Zak mumbled as he rolled onto his side.

"Zak!" Lark screeched as he pounced on his lover, shaking his broad, tanned shoulders mercilessly.

"I'm sure annoying, little sadomasochists were outlawed by the Geneva Convention a few years back," Zak grumbled, but there was no anger in his voice. There never was.

"Just as well I'm neither annoying nor little then," Lark retorted with a mock pout and a sniff of disdain.

He didn't object to the charge of sadomasochism, however. He really did enjoy winding Zak up far too much to deny it, and he absolutely loved Zak's punishments afterwards. He did, however, relent just a little on the physical abuse now that Zak was beginning to sound coherent. Lark knew it wouldn't be long before he got what he wanted.

"Oh! You're definitely little," Zak muttered into his pillow.

"Am not!"

"Are too!"

"Am not!"

Lark could hear the smile in Zak's voice but knew his lover was fighting it as they continued back and forth with the familiar banter. He felt his heart swell a little more with overwhelming love.

"I'm not little where it counts," he insisted playfully, thrusting his hips forward so Zak could feel the growing bulge of his erection through the thin sheet.

Zak growled, then rolled over with a loud roar to pin Lark to the mattress beneath him in a squealing, giggling mess.

Lark squirmed and thrashed, but when Zak swooped in to claim his laughing mouth, in a hard, possessive kiss, Lark surrendered enthusiastically. Zak's kisses were far too good to miss a moment of them.

Tongues tangled and caressed across each other, probing deeply then gently licking at the tender, bruised flesh and running lightly over smooth white teeth. Eyes closed in bliss and moans of appreciation began to fill the room as retaliation turned to rapture and red-hot need.

Slowly, they pulled away from each other, and Lark couldn't hold in a soft whimper at the loss.

"Are you trying to distract me?" he panted, staring up into Zak's handsome face and tracing his fingers down the dark stubbly fur of his cheek.

"Is it working?" Zak asked; his light peridot-green eyes flecked with golden brown smouldered with a heady combination of mischief and lust. All traces of sleepy man were now completely gone.

"Maybe," Lark replied with a saucy grin. "But I'm really hungry, Zak," he added, raising his head to lick suggestively at Zak's lips again.

"Mmmm...me too," Zak agreed as he leaned in for another drugging kiss. "What do you think we should do about that?"

Lark bit at his bottom lip as he pretended to consider his options. But after barely a second of teasing, he began to push insistently on his lover's shoulders until the much bigger man took the hint and settled onto his back in the middle of the mattress.

Lark took the time to push the light cotton sheet off completely and admire Zak's beautiful, naked body. He let his gaze travel down firm, defined muscles before straddling rock-hard thighs. He admired Zak's bare, tanned flesh and was once again eternally grateful for the man's predilection for nude sunbathing. Laid out like this — a veritable feast for the senses — Zak was magnificent.

Reaching out, Lark traced Zak's well shaped pectorals and tweaked both hard, pebbled nipples. He ran his fingers lightly through the soft mat of hair that grew across Zak's broad chest — such a contrast to his own smooth torso — then followed it down over his firm, rippled belly as it trailed in a teasing path to disappear beneath him where he sat over Zak like a conquering hero.

No matter how many times he saw the man naked like this, Lark could never bring himself to believe Zak was real. He always found himself needing to touch and caress. To reassure himself that Zak was there with him.

When Zak groaned and thrust up against him, Lark chuckled and shifted a little to let Zak's rigid cock, trapped beneath him, run up along the smooth silk of his sleep pants and stroke across his inner thigh.

Well, that certainly felt real, Lark thought, grinning like a fool when he saw the small trail of pre-cum that was left behind in a thin, wet line across the silk of his pants and the jewel-beaded thread of cum that now connected him to Zak's thick, uncut cock.

"Naughty boy," he chided playfully, "you got me all wet."

"Oh, baby!" Zak rumbled back in a deep, husky voice that sent a shiver down Lark's spine. "Let me make it up to you and help you out of those messy things."

With that, Zak began to slip the material off Lark's hips with his broad, calloused hands. Lark didn't waste any time in lifting up and helping him remove the offending pants, quickly returning to his position over Zak's thighs and delighting in the feel of their cocks meeting and rubbing together—happily sharing their pre-cum as the lust and need grew between them.

Lowering himself to lay over the much bigger man, Lark joined their lips together for another long, passionate kiss. The sensation of Zak's broad hands travelling up and down his back, caressing him as their tongues danced and mated between their mouths, had him moaning and undulating helplessly in seconds.

No way could Lark stop himself from rubbing and thrusting against Zak when he touched him like this. His body simply refused to be restrained. But Lark had plans for this morning, and he knew if he didn't find some control soon, he was going to miss his chance.

Not that there wouldn't be other opportunities. In fact, he sincerely hoped that this morning would lead to a whole new enthusiasm and repertoire for them to explore in their lovemaking. But first, he had to get them both back on the right track.

Using every ounce of willpower he possessed, Lark gradually managed to bring the kiss to an end and pulled away. For a moment, all he could do was pant for breath as he tried to get a grip on his runaway libido. Then he looked down at Zak and saw the slightly unfocused, confused look in his eye, and he couldn't help but grin wickedly.

This was going to be so much fun. In fact, it already was, he realised. He loved the wary look of expectation that entered his lover's eyes as Zak cocked an eyebrow, waiting to see what he would do next. He was thrilled with the idea that he could still surprise his lover. He had to admit it was getting harder and harder to do.

They'd known each other practically forever. In fact, Lark couldn't remember a time without Zak. And he loved that about them. He knew everything there was to know about the other man — what he liked, how he liked it and every sensitive, sensual spot Zak possessed. And in return Zak knew all his secrets, too. It was something that warmed Lark to the very centre of his being, and he never wanted to lose it. But lately he was starting to feel like there was something…missing. Like there was something more they needed. It was…unsettling.

Lark ruthlessly pushed the uncomfortable thoughts away. He didn't want them to intrude on this time. It was one of the reasons he had bargained so fiercely with Rio to open up the restaurant today — so he could have some quality time with Zak.

He certainly wasn't anywhere near brave enough to ask Zak if he was feeling the same sense that something was missing. All he knew was he needed time to love on his man and reassure himself that everything was going to be okay between them. That whatever it was he was feeling, they would get through it together. Just like they always had.

"You know, I bought you something special, big boy," Lark announced with a playful wiggle of his eyebrows.

He watched with amusement as a comical mix of curiosity and concern crossed Zak's face. Ah! He loved that look. It seemed like an age since he had managed to put it on his lover's face. Somewhere deep inside, Lark felt a sudden easing of his anxiety — knowing that he could still do it after all these years was very reassuring.

"You did?" Zak asked hesitantly.

"Mmmm...I did. Want to see?" Lark fought hard to hold in his laughter as his cautious lover warily nodded his head.

"Okay."

Leaning up over Zak, Lark reached for the top drawer of his bedside table and pulled out a black rectangular box with a bright red ribbon tied elegantly around it. A nice match to the contents actually, he mused, settling back down over Zak's warm, firm body like a cat reclining on its favourite napping spot. Which he supposed was a fair analogy — Zak was his favourite napping spot.

He brought the box down to rest on Zak's broad, furry chest and waited.

Zak eyed the box suspiciously, shifting his gaze to focus on Lark for a moment, then back to the box rising and falling innocently on his chest as if it might bite him. Finally, Zak reached for it and began pulling gently at one tail of the ribbon.

Lark felt like bouncing on the spot with excitement as he eagerly awaited Zak's reaction to his gift. This, he decided, was so much fun he'd have to make sure they got another picnic day again very soon.

Finally, Zak worked off the lid, and Lark had the satisfaction of seeing his lover's eyes almost bug out of his head as he lifted the bright red, glittery butt plug from its bed of snowy white satin.

Lark finally gave in to the temptation and began to bounce softly, feeling their cocks riding over one another with the sudden movement and wanting more. More action. More play. More, now, damn it!

"Do you like it?" Lark asked enthusiastically.

"It's ahh…"

"It's a butt plug."

"I know what it is, Lark! But…ahh…is it for me or —"

"Of course it's for you!" Lark cried, snatching the moulded red plug from Zak's hands. He reached for the lube that always sat out beside the bed. "You're going to love it. Trust me. I know we haven't really been into exploring this sort of thing before, but I just know it's going to feel so good." Applying a liberal amount of lube and smoothing it evenly over the plug, Lark waggled it enthusiastically in Zak's face. "I'm going to just blow your mind with this, baby."

Zak looked less than convinced as he eyed the modestly sized sex toy.

Lark forced himself to calm down for a moment in the face of his lover's obvious uncertainty. Leaning forward, he gently touched their lips together in a sweet, tender caress.

"Trust me, sweetheart," Lark said, gazing into Zak's eyes.

"I do, Lark. Always," Zak replied quickly with a serious intensity that shot straight through Lark like electricity — so much love, so much faith.

Lark touched Zak's lips again, trying to convey all the love and care he had in his heart. He'd never do anything to hurt Zak. Never in a million years.

"Good, boy," Lark suddenly quipped, breaking the intense moment with a cheeky grin.

Lark was delighted when he heard Zak reply with an easy chuckle. Reassured that Zak was ready to explore, Lark began to wiggle down his gorgeous lover's body.

Zak adjusted himself so Lark could kneel between his spread thighs and Lark paused for a moment to stare—savouring the moment of seeing the most intimate part of his lover.

Lark loved the fact Zak could still amaze him sometimes almost as much as he loved the idea of surprising the man. Being willing to explore something new like this, letting Lark see him all vulnerable and exposed...it was the ultimate in trust and acceptance. Especially for someone as naturally cautious and reserved as Zak.

Lark thought back to how hard it had been in the beginning. They'd been together like this for nearly six years now. But they'd been in each other's lives a lot longer than that, and becoming lovers had been a long, difficult struggle. For both of them.

Fuck, it had been hard—waiting until he'd turned eighteen, convincing Zak that they belonged together, confronting their parents. For a long time, he thought they would never make it work. But now, after six years, the two of them finally seemed to have made it.

And they'd pretty much explored every inch of each other, too. They had fucked—man, that first night had been something else—fingered, jerked, blown, and rimmed each other endlessly. But, strangely enough, they'd never tried sex toys.

Maybe there just hadn't been enough room in their lives for anything else up until now. Maybe it was his own fault for not taking the initiative. Heaven knew the sensible, straight-laced man he loved wasn't likely to instigate even the mildest of kinky play. Not that

Zak wasn't passionate and amazingly competent with what he'd been born with, but Lark knew he would need to be the one to lead if they were going to expand their horizons in this area of their lives.

And more and more Lark felt that was what they needed. He finally felt settled and comfortable in his skin, in his relationship with Zak, and he wanted to explore his newfound confidence. To try new things and see what happened.

Pulling himself away from the rambling thoughts in his head as Zak started to shift — apparently uncomfortable with the continued scrutiny — Lark reached out for his lover. He lightly caressed his fingers down from Zak's balls, along the tender flesh of his perineum and around the small puckered entrance of his ass. As he did, he felt Zak shiver and tense slightly under his gentle caress.

"Well, this isn't going to work," he said lightly, running his fingers over Zak's tense hole again.

"What?" Zak demanded anxiously.

"You're all uptight. I think you need a little something before we start."

Without allowing Zak time to process the words, Lark leaned in and swiped his tongue over Zak's tight hole, giggling when the man nearly shot up off the bed.

"Aaahhhh! Shit, Lark! A little more warning, huh?" Zak chastised as he slowly relaxed back down on the mattress.

"No way! Life's too short to worry about warnings," Lark grinned unrepentantly.

"You should come with a warning," Zak groused in a low murmur.

Lark licked him firmly again before stabbing his stiffened tongue into Zak's hole in retaliation —

delighting to the sudden cry he dragged from his lover.

Oh, yeah. So much fun!

Enthusiastically, Lark began to work at Zak, trying to loosen the tight muscles so they could really begin to play. Zak squirmed and moaned under his questing tongue, but gradually his hole relaxed until Lark could add a finger, then a second and third — gently scissored and explored with them until he was sure Zak was ready for his gift.

"That's it. Just relax, baby. I've got you," Lark crooned, as he ran the tip of the plug over and around Zak's now-eager hole before applying gentle, firm pressure and watching in awe as the rounded head of the plug disappeared into his lover's hot body.

"Beautiful, Zak. So beautiful."

Leaning forward, he gently took Zak's cock into his mouth as he continued to work the plug slowly in. Using a teasing in-and-out slide, so that with each thrust a little more was taken into Zak's body before being pulled away, Lark managed to stretch out the pleasure for several long minutes. Thrusting and retreating, all the while lazily sucking and licking at the thick cock in his mouth.

Lark moaned in pleasure. So good.

Finally, Lark pushed the plug all the way home and began a deep, slow sucking while he rotated the plug in place.

"Ah! Fuck!" Zak cried, thrusting up into Lark's mouth desperately.

The smile that formed on Lark's lips broke the tight suction of his mouth around Zak's cock and gave his lover a brief moment of reprieve to gather his thoughts.

"Get your ass around here now," Zak growled, "or you're gonna be missing out."

Lark could hear how seriously turned on Zak was in that moment and knew the man wasn't joking. If Zak came like this, he'd be way too blissed out to reciprocate for a while, and Lark didn't feel like going solo right now. Not when he had a hot man offering his mouth right there under him. That would just be fucking stupid. And one thing Lark prided himself on was not being stupid.

He quickly swung himself around into position — with his knees on either side of Zak's head and his mouth still working up and down the thick shaft held securely between his lips. His own aching cock so was rigid, Zak had to reach up and pull it down to his lips from where it bobbed happily against Lark's flat, smooth belly.

The first touch of Zak's tongue swiping at the thin drops of pre-cum leaking from his slit had Lark moaning and tensing — fighting for control around Zak's shaft. If he weren't so comfortable and secure in the love they shared, Lark might have been embarrassed by how quickly Zak could make him come. As it was, Lark just focussed all his energy on renewing his strong, insistent suckling of the cock in his mouth and began to manipulate the plug in Zak's ass again.

The strong suction quickly dragged more and more pre-cum out of Zak's rock-hard cock. It coated Lark's tongue and throat, and he moaned helplessly at the unique flavour that was all Zak. Then he felt the brush of fingers over his balls, trailing up the soft, tender skin behind and over his clenching hole.

He wasn't going to last, he realised. He needed Zak to come. Now!

Desperately, Lark fought down his gag reflex to take Zak's cock as far as possible down into his throat. He felt Zak buck beneath him just as his own shaft began to throb in release. Miraculously, they came together, swallowing down each other's spunk as they shared an intense, mutual orgasm.

"Love you," he heard Zak croak beneath him several minutes later when they had both finally managed to catch their breath slightly.

"Love you, too," he whispered back, adding a soft kiss to the inner thigh he rested against as he slowly came down from his euphoric high.

There was no way he would ever lose what he had with this man, Lark vowed. Just no way. No matter what he had to do to keep them together he would hold onto Zak until his very last breath.

Chapter Two

Brody watched Lark—the cute, bubbly little blond he'd been directed to when he'd walked in asking for work—flipping through his resume. He tried not to let his nervousness show. The man might mistake nervous for shifty, and shifty could cost him a job. Brody couldn't afford that.

Actually, right now he couldn't afford anything.

This really was his last chance, he acknowledged grimly. He had absolutely no money left. The rent was paid up for another two weeks, but after that, he and Wolf would be out on their ear. And worse still, there was no food left—Wolf had eaten the last tin of baked beans for dinner. The cupboard was quite literally bare. If he didn't get work here tonight, he was going to have to take drastic action.

Brody fought hard to control his breathing. He knew that if he started turning tricks, he'd be risking everything. It was a steep, slippery slope to disaster after that. And once he started down, there was almost no hope he would ever be able to climb his way back up and make things right again. He couldn't jeopardise everything he'd worked so hard for over the last few years like that. He and Wolf had moved halfway across the country to escape that sort of thing and leave that life behind forever. But there would be no second chances. Not this time.

Trying to distract himself from his desperate and depressing thoughts, Brody surveyed the dining room while he waited. The restaurant—Sandpipers—was small but had that warm, intimate feeling he knew people loved.

That was good, he reassured himself. If the restaurant was well liked, people would come back. And if people kept coming back, then the owners would have enough money to hire him on. Brody found himself crossing his fingers and hoping to catch a break for once.

Gazing around, he took in the huge, rough, wooden posts that broke up the otherwise open floor plan. He admired the large potted palms scattered about and the whitewashed walls lined with seascapes depicting the beach just a short walk down the esplanade. It was all very tastefully done to be neither fish-and-chip-shop casual, nor fine dining intense.

Brody could imagine couples and families dropping in after a stroll along the boardwalk, or lovers enjoying the evening breeze and the flickering candlelit centre pieces over a romantic dinner for two.

Focusing again on the man in front of him, Brody tried to work out exactly what Lark's story might be. He'd introduced himself as the co-owner and front of house manager. But he really didn't look old enough.

Propped up on a stool, leaning back against the long bar with one foot resting on the cross-brace and one dangling free—because he was too short to touch the floor—Lark looked even younger than Brody's own twenty-two years. Yet, as the wait-staff and barmen moved around them preparing for the evening opening, it was obvious that he was definitely the one in charge. People constantly interrupted to ask questions or get direction.

While Brody continued to watch, Lark began to play with the pen in his fingers and bounce his foot against the stool's cross-brace, a movement that made his whole leg wiggle rapidly. It was as if his body simply refused to stay still, even while he was concentrating on something else.

Man, he's cute. Brody shifted and tried not to stare. But it was hard to look away. The man's ruffled, pale blond hair hung forward slightly, shadowing his eyes. It made Brody want to reach out and brush it away so he could see the amazing dark blue orbs looking back at him again.

Clamping down on his runaway thoughts, Brody tore his gaze away. He was just overanxious, he reassured himself. This was the first time in days of job-hunting that anyone had actually asked to see his resume. It wasn't much, but it gave him a small thrill of hope—one his experiences had taught him he should smother immediately.

This Lark—and what sort of a name is that anyway, it's way too cute and perky—might just want to dangle me a little longer before giving me the brush off.

But chancing another glance over at the man, Brody didn't think so. Lark didn't seem like the type. In fact, when he had first met him, Brody had thought the man was going to give him a hug.

Not that he would have minded necessarily. Lark was amazingly attractive, and watching him, Brody couldn't help smiling. He seemed to be the sort of person people gravitated to and liked automatically – the sort of person who always had a happy smile and a kind word and a...hug. It set up a little ache of longing deep inside that Brody really didn't want to acknowledge or examine too closely.

Thinking about what it would feel like to have the smaller man wrap his arms around him, Brody suddenly found himself watching Lark's sweet bow-shaped, pale pink lips and wondering what they would taste like. Brody looked away again as he felt himself flush with embarrassment.

What the fuck am I thinking? This man was obviously one of the bosses around here, and this could be Brody's one big chance to finally get a job. And there was nothing to suggest Lark would be interested anyway. The man co-owned a restaurant for fuck's sake. Why would he give someone like Brody a second look? He might not even be gay.

Although, on that front, Brody would be rather surprised. His gaydar was pinging like mad. His cock was half hard just looking at the man and Brody couldn't help but imagine all sorts of delicious things they could do together.

Yet it also made Brody start to ponder the smaller man's story. Since it looked like they were about the same age, he had to wonder how Lark had managed to be in a position to co-own a restaurant already. Maybe it was a family business. Or maybe he had some rich boyfriend. Maybe that was who the other owner was.

Yeah! Well done, Brody, you dumb schmuck.

Great. It would be just his luck to not only be lusting after the boss, but quite probably a man who was the other boss's boyfriend as well.

"So, when can you start?" Lark suddenly asked as he looked up and threw the slim resume onto the bar over his shoulder like the piece of worthless crap it was.

"What?" Brody asked, startled out of his self-recriminations by the abrupt job offer. "I mean, I...really?"

But if Brody had been shocked by the job offer, he was even more staggered by the radiant smile the smaller man turned on him as he chuckled softly — happiness and pleasure twinkling in Lark's dark blue eyes.

"Yes, really. I mean, it's only a kitchen hand's position, but you seem to have done the work before, and I'm sure the others will let you know pretty quickly about anything else you need to learn."

"Oh! That's... Now! I mean, I can start right now if you want me to," Brody stammered. The chance of a paycheque even one day sooner was too good an opportunity to pass up.

"Cool. Come on. I'll introduce you to the rest of the gang."

With that, Lark grabbed his hand and tugged Brody along behind him as he literally seemed to bounce through the still-deserted dining room — leading him through a set of swinging doors and into the kitchen.

"Gentlemen! I come bearing gifts," Lark announced grandly as he dragged Brody into the room. "As promised, one kitchen hand!"

"About fucking time," grumbled a tall, dark haired man in a white chef's tunic without looking up from the carrot he chopped with efficient strokes.

"Now, Dave, language, please. We're trying to make a good impression," Lark admonished playfully in a light, musical voice.

Dave flipped him off casually, almost without pausing his rapid knife work.

"Everyone, this is Brody. He'll be starting tonight, then working Thursday through Sunday from now on."

"Sucker," a skinny man with his dark brown curly hair pulled back under a black bandana grunted from the back corner.

"So, you've meant Mr. Potty-mouth, Dave, over there." Lark indicated the man still cutting up vegetables. "Mr. Sarcastic is Andy. Then there's Rio and Gus, head chef and mains respectively. Saturday night, we have all hands on deck, as you can see, but normally we rotate through our days off during the week. So it's good you came tonight, you get to meet everyone at the same time this way."

"Yeah! That and the fact we're going to have a fucking truckload of pans because someone decided to cater a cocktail party on the deck as well as open for dinner," Dave said—again without looking up from his chopping block.

Lark ignored Dave's comment completely this time.

"Everyone has Monday off at the moment because it's just too slow to justify opening, but that might change if things pick up—so there could be a chance for some more work later on in the season.

"That would be great," Brody hurried to assure the man, wanting him to know he would always take any work they wanted to give him.

"So what else..." Lark wondered aloud as he gazed around the room. "Oh! Of course. Uniforms. Have you got some of your own?"

Brody shook his head, hoping it wasn't going to be a deal breaker. He simply couldn't afford a set of uniforms at the moment. Or probably any time soon for that matter.

"That's okay. I'm pretty sure we've got a spare couple of sets you can use, back in the office. The last guy left them when he ran off to who knows where. He was about your size. And I guess we better get onto the paperwork too. Then you can come back in and get familiar with the place before it starts getting busy."

Brody felt a little overwhelmed by how fast everything was moving all of a sudden. As Lark led him towards a door on the far side of the room with the word OFFICE printed on it in neat, gold letters, he could only nod dumbly and follow along behind.

With his brain refusing to co-operate and the intense smell of food reminding him he hadn't eaten today — making him feel slightly dizzy — Brody concentrated on Lark and hoped he didn't make a fool of himself. The bright little man couldn't have been more than five-foot-four in boots, he realised as he tried not to stare at the firm ass encased in tight black pants that flexed and tensed in front of him.

Suddenly, Lark looked back over his shoulder — grinning as if he knew exactly what Brody was doing. His bright white teeth and mischievous blue eyes made Brody's heart stutter out a funny little beat for a second before settling into an even, but slightly faster rhythm.

Just as Brody was sure he was going to die of embarrassment for being caught ogling his new boss's ass, someone stepped out of the office in front of Lark and the two of them collided heavily.

As Lark bounced off the man's broad chest, Brody stepped forward to try and save him from falling on the hard kitchen floor. But the bigger man had already reached out to pull Lark back—wrapping large, muscular arms round him. Brody found himself caught up in the impromptu hug—pressed up tight against Lark's back.

For a moment the three of them just stood together, frozen in place with Lark sandwiched between them. Then the man holding Lark protectively against his chest chuckled.

"You okay, baby?" he asked.

Brody found himself mesmerised by the man's face. His eyes—not green or brown, but some sort of indescribable mixture of the two, framed by sinfully long, dark lashes—were breathtaking. As was the ultra-short dark hair that covered his head and shadowed his firm, square jaw. Brody couldn't stop watching the man's beautifully shaped lips as they moved to speak to Lark.

"Oh! Yes. Very okay," Lark replied in a slightly husky, amused voice. "This is nice."

As Lark wiggled between them suggestively, Brody suddenly realised how closely he was standing and hastily stepped back. The flush that had begun when he got caught ogling Lark's ass burst into full flame on his cheeks in an instant.

Man, what is wrong with me today, Brody wondered, thoroughly mortified by his overactive libido.

"How disappointing," Lark sighed with a hint of laughter in his voice as he patted the impressive, muscular chest in front of him.

Brody pushed away the sudden desire to be in Lark's shoes as Lark turned back to face him.

"Zak, I'd like you to meet Brody McAllister, our new kitchen hand. Brody, this is Zak—co-owner and resident hunk."

"Behave, trouble," Zak warned with a chuckle as he bumped Lark gently with his hip—which only made Lark laugh out loud.

Brody fought against the sudden erection that threatened to tent his pants and shame him. A strange sensation—something almost like jealousy—swept over him as he watched the two share a smile of unmistakable love and happiness.

Then Lark stepped aside and Zak stretched out his hand in greeting, forcing Brody to pay attention and return the gesture.

"Nice to meet you," Zak rumbled in a deep, penetrating voice that seemed to vibrate right through Brody.

The man's eyes were boring into him now, and Brody found it difficult to let go of his warm, calloused hand when the handshake needed to come to an end, or become something more intimate.

Man, I need to get laid. It was as if having the all-consuming pressure to find a job suddenly lifted from his shoulders had sent it all straight to his pants. His cock was certainly stressing that it needed some action. And apparently it was happy to pick out likely candidates for him to consider—left, right and centre.

* * * *

Zak pulled back his hand from the warm, firm handshake and took a moment to look over their newest employee. He was a bit surprised at how disappointed he was that he had to release the man's hand. Brody had nice hands and the contact had felt good.

Actually, now that he looked, Brody was really kind of cute. A little on the skinny side perhaps, but those pale blue eyes that looked away shyly...and the lean, but very masculine frame...mmm, very nice. Brody would be just Zak's type, if he weren't already well and truly taken with Lark.

Zak flexed his fingers and thought again about the way Brody's hand had felt resting in his own. He had a thing for hands. There was nothing like the feel of a man's hands moving over skin – touching, exploring, bringing all the other senses to focus on the intimate contact between two people.

Mmmm, yes... Zak struggled to turn his wicked grin into a friendly smile. After closing tonight, he would need to do some serious tactile loving with Lark. If only Lark had more than two hands.

Suddenly, Zak found himself thinking about what it would be like to have Brody's hands moving over him, too. His cock began to fill until it caught at an odd angle and throbbed painfully in the confines of his pants.

Well, that was a stupid fucking thing to think. He took a step back and pulled Lark in front of him to hide his erection.

Unfortunately, as Zak discreetly tried to adjust himself, Lark looked around with a slightly confused expression. Zak felt a slight flush creep up his neck. Fuck, nothing like getting sprung.

Zak continued to force a smile as he tried desperately to will his erection away. He hoped Lark hadn't noticed his ill-timed reaction and jumped to the wrong conclusion. Sure he found Brody attractive, but he loved Lark. Not just loved, but – adored and worshipped. He wanted Lark in that forever-and-always, soppy kind of way he would never admit out loud. There was no other man he would rather spend the rest of his life with.

Okay, so maybe he didn't mind looking at the man in front of them, and maybe he inspired one or two wicked thoughts. But that was just a nice little fantasy. Eye candy. A daydream. He shouldn't be feeling uncomfortable or…guilty.

"I was actually just bringing Brody in to you, Zak," Lark was saying while Zak tried to sort out his confusing thoughts and emotions. "He needs to get paperwork done so he can start tonight, and I promised him those spare jackets Ryan left behind before he did a runner."

"Sure. Um…I think they're hanging in the far locker," Zak murmured, hoping to make a quick get away to relieve himself of his embarrassing, not so little problem. Willing his erection away just wasn't working.

"And the paperwork?"

"Top drawer of the filing cabinet."

Damn. Lark was hopeless when it came to navigating his way around the filing system. There went his opportunity to high tail it out of here and get his unruly cock back in line. Zak couldn't, in all good conscience, abandon Lark when he knew his little lover was going to need help.

"Come on, Brody. Let's see what we can dig up."

Zak watched as Lark took Brody by the hand and led him into the office.

Oh, shit! Zak felt a rush of panic as he struggled to tear his gaze away from the two of them walking away together hand-in-hand. The images that filled his mind—how perfect the two of them would look naked, touching each other and writhing over clean sheets—was intensely erotic, and equally intensely disturbing.

This was bad. Because as hard as he'd been moments before, just watching Brody holding hands with Lark nearly had him coming in his pants.

What the hell was wrong with him? There wasn't anything remotely sexual about what they were doing, and he didn't know the younger man from Adam. But watching the two men together turned him on like nothing else.

Lark, with his small, almost delicate frame, and Brody, with his taller, more average build and darker hair, complemented each other beautifully. The two of them looked good together. Whereas Zak sometimes felt too big and oafish around Lark, Brody was just the right size to hold Lark without having to worry about crushing him.

And wasn't that supposed to stir up all sorts of jealous feelings in him—the thought of another man holding his Lark? Instead, Zak found himself wondering what the two of them would look like naked together. The whole idea would be completely fucked up—if the image weren't so damn hot.

"Hey! Zak. Can you come over here a minute?" Lark called out to him from the filing cabinet by the far wall, where Brody stood patiently beside him.

No problem, Zak thought cynically. The trick was going to be not coming if he joined the two of them.

"Sure, what do you need?" he finally managed, in a reasonably calm voice that he was actually quite proud of, given his state at the moment.

"I'm after the 'new employees' thingy, but I'm not having any luck. Can you help me out?"

Oh, fuck! Somebody upstairs hates me, Zak thought as he struggled to get his mind out of the gutter. It was going to be a really long afternoon.

* * * *

Lark suppressed a grin. Zak hadn't actually groaned at the subtle tease he'd let slip into the request, but after so many years together he didn't have to—Lark could quite clearly see the heat and desire clouding his lover's eyes.

And, wow, it was hot.

The way Zak's gaze focussed and caressed over them as Lark stood beside Brody by the filing cabinet. The way his lover's hands tensed and relaxed as if he desperately wanted to touch them—to run his big hands over heated flesh and investigate every inch of them. Lark felt his own lust kick into high gear at the mere thought of it.

Who would have thought Zak—quiet, serious-minded Zak—could be tempted by the idea of a threesome? That he could be led so easily into exploring the wonderful world of kink? It almost made him wish he'd thought to buy his man sex toys years ago! It looked like he'd created a monster—and, man, he couldn't wait to ride it!

Beside him, he felt Brody shift nervously—no doubt trying to hide the impressive bulge in the front of his pants. He didn't embarrass the man by pointing out he'd long since given the game away. Well...at least not too obviously. Teasing Brody a little wasn't something he could completely forgo.

"Oops! Don't worry, I think I found it," Lark announced, dragging out the paperwork he'd been looking for with a flourish. "I don't know how I missed it. Is it just me or is this thing getting bigger all the time?"

Both Brody and Zak blushed.

Oh! The two of them were just too adorable.

Taking Brody by the hand—mainly so he could watch Zak's reaction again—Lark led him over to the desk. "Come on, we should get started. This could take a while, and I for one have much better things I can think of doing with my time."

"Um...okay. I just hope I've got everything you're going to need," Brody replied, eyeing the stack of paperwork apprehensively.

"Oh! Don't worry," Lark said, patting Brody's knee reassuringly—really, it was reassurance. "I'm sure we'll work it all out."

"I'll...um...I'll just go out and help the...ah...the guys in the kitchen," Zak stammered—still watching them intently.

"Okay. But don't go too far away, honey. I'm definitely going to need you." Lark turned to Brody—who was still flushed right to the tips of his ears. "I'm terrible at all this paperwork stuff."

Brody nodded, shifting in his seat.

Things had certainly taken a distinctly interesting turn since Brody had stepped into the restaurant this afternoon. Lark couldn't wait to see what the rest of the day had in store for them.

Chapter Three

Zak felt the beads of sweat start to form and slowly trickle down his temple. It had nothing to do with the heat in the kitchen and everything to do with the heat he felt radiating off Brody's body as they stood side-by-side at the counter.

Zak was trying to show Brody what they required in the way of simple prep work at the restaurant, while at the same time trying not to show the other man how hard his cock got whenever Brody came anywhere near him. It wasn't easy. The close proximity was doing a real number on his libido.

Yet the excuses Zak had come up with for being the one to show Brody the ropes were numerous, if somewhat flimsy. Someone needed to take the time and do it properly. The regular chefs were too busy. He wanted to refresh his skills and stretch his culinary muscles after being buried under the mountain of paperwork the restaurant seemed to generate for so long.

Zak snorted. That last one was the biggest crock of all. There were usually plenty of opportunities to keep his skills up, either doing holiday relief or during the busier weekends they sometimes catered. And he certainly wasn't likely to forget how to make a few vegetable garnishes. He had worked in kitchens since his mid-teens.

No, the simple truth was Zak wanted to take Brody under his wing and protect him. He didn't want any of the others getting too close or worst still, messing with the quiet, slightly reserved man. Kitchens were notorious for rough play with new recruits, and Zak didn't want Brody to have to deal with any of that crap. Something told him that was the last thing Brody needed right now.

Zak resisted the urge to shake his head at himself. He'd spent far too much time in the kitchen satisfying his protective urge towards Brody recently. It really had to stop. The paperwork was mounting up and none of the others had really shown any special interest in Brody either way.

Some small part of his brain acknowledged that he had enjoyed the opportunity to get to know Brody a little better though. He really was a great guy. Quiet and hard working. And quick, too. Most of the simple tricks and techniques Zak had been showing him, Brody picked up within a couple of attempts. Anything he got wrong, he would simply study, put aside and try again without any fuss or bother.

Zak watched as Brody put the finishing touches to the radish rosette he'd been so diligently concentrating on. He seemed to have a natural flare for presentation. He was an excellent addition to the kitchen.

Reaching up and resting his hand on the back of Brody's neck without thinking, Zak gently squeezed the column affectionately before petting the fine, soft, strands of hair he found there.

"Well done, Brody. That's excellent."

Brody turned his head, a radiant smile making his face shine with pleasure at the praise, and Zak felt his stomach flip over as their eyes met.

Zak instantly pulled away, horrified by his reaction to the man. Fuck, this isn't happening. It just was *not* happening.

The blood froze in his veins as he struggled for something to say. Something to make it stop. Or go away. Or better yet, both.

He loved Lark. Nothing could change that. Nothing could come between them. Lark was everything Zak had ever wanted. And nothing, absolutely nothing had changed, Zak reassured himself. So why was he so intensely attracted to another man? How could this be happening?

Fuck! He had to figure out a way to stay cool and distant. Now! He had to get some control.

Drawing away, Zak straightened up and squared his shoulders.

"Very good, Brody. You did well. I think you're ready to handle it on your own from here." Zak was proud of the cool, professional tone of his voice. Not so proud of the way Brody snapped back as if he'd been struck. Hard.

Zak watched as Brody turned a deep, dark red before quickly looking away.

"Thanks," Brody mumbled, picking up the small knife he had been working with and reaching for another radish.

Yes. Professional, that was the key. Zak knew he had to come up with some control, because the only other option was to let Brody go, and he sure as hell couldn't do that either. It wouldn't be fair, just because he couldn't stop lusting after the man, to force him out.

The real hell of it all was that Zak really liked Brody. He was a good man. He was kind and unassuming. And yet he seemed to have no concept of how attractive he was. He certainly didn't deserve to be treated like a piece of meat—which is all Zak could offer. It could never be any more than that.

Could it?

Just as Zak thought it was probably time to make a break for it and bury himself under the pile of paperwork awaiting him in the office, Lark walked in. Zak braced himself for the flare of panic. For the shame and self-recrimination he was sure he should feel. But it never came. It was beyond strange. But there it was.

Zak stared at Lark for a moment. Trying to comprehend what was going on. He didn't even feel a momentary twinge of guilt. He just felt...overwhelming relief. Lark was here. Lark's presence made it all right—perfect in fact.

Zak's heart eased and filled with warmth. Lark would always make him feel this way. There was no reason to worry. His breath hitched as an unexpected grin stretched his lips.

"Hey, short-stuff." Zak stepped up to meet Lark and wrapped his arms around his lover.

"Huh!" Lark huffed playfully. "That's not what you said to me this morning."

Zak found himself swept up in the playfulness his heart was so light. "Well, you know what they say — never kick a man while he's going down."

Lark chuckled, shoving Zak's shoulder affectionately. "They do not!"

Zak pulled Lark back in and let the smaller man's proximity soothe and smother his agitation completely. It felt so good — knowing nothing had changed between them. In fact, it made him a little giddy and more demonstrative than he might otherwise have been in the kitchen. But Zak didn't care. He just wanted to breathe in the moment and be grateful.

"They should, you know. I think it's excellent advice to live by."

"Mmm...you may have a point there." Lark lifted himself up on the tips of his toes to peck Zak lightly on the lips.

Yes, this was it. This was good and safe and home.

* * * *

Brody watched as Zak and Lark enjoyed their playful little interlude and felt an overwhelming desire to be a part of it. What would it be like to be in a relationship like that? To have the love and easy companionship that the two men so obviously shared?

"You all done for a bit?" Lark asked Zak with a faint trace of husky promise in his voice that Brody found completely irresistible.

"Yep. I'm all yours," Zak replied.

Brody found himself mesmerised by the exchange. By the look in their eyes and the way they touched each other — so freely, so easily.

"Oh! I like the sound of that. You okay if I take him away from you..." Without warning, Lark turned to face Brody, his voice trailing off when he caught him openly staring at the two of them.

Probably slack jawed and drooling, knowing my luck, Brody thought as he quickly looked away, feeling his cheeks burst into flame with embarrassment for the second time in ten minutes. *Damn!*

Fumbling for a random vegetable to concentrate on, Brody quickly selected a carrot and set to work preparing it. He tried not to notice the silence filling the void between them all, but it became increasingly difficult.

Finally, Lark spoke again, his voice still whisky-rough. "Wow! I was going to ask if you were okay with me taking Zak away from you for a while, Brody. But—"

"It's fine. I got this under control now," Brody quickly replied, refusing to look away from the chopping board—he'd probably take his fingers off if he did right now.

"Yeah. Brody's a quick study. He's fine," Zak added.

"But—"

"Come on, Lark. I've got something to show you." Zak started dragging Lark away before the smaller man could make any further protest or an excuse to stay.

Brody was extremely grateful. Okay, perhaps a little disappointed too, but mostly grateful.

Stilling the knife in his hand, he closed his eyes for a moment and took a deep, cleansing breath. He was pretty sure he should quit.

Walking away and avoiding the trouble his intense attraction to the men was sure to cause seemed like the smart thing to do. Unfortunately, he simply couldn't afford to do that. This job was the answer to a desperate man's prays. Someone just seemed to have gone a bit overboard with the generosity—having two guys like Lark and Zak as his bosses seemed...well, almost cruel to be honest.

But then, maybe everything would be all right now. Brody had felt the change in Zak. He'd sensed the instant the man had drawn away from him—becoming cold and distant. Not mean, just...professional. In a lot of ways it was a huge relief.

Now, if only he could imitate that calm control. He should be able to keep his interactions between himself and the two men polite but cool.

Cool was good. Cool might have some chance of damping down the heat he felt in his pants every time he was in the same room with them. Of course, getting Lark to agree to the plan was starting to look like a long shot. Brody only had his observations of the smaller man to go on, but he definitely didn't come across as the sort of person to take a step back, or miss even the slightest opportunity or encouragement.

Watching Lark had become one of his favourite pastimes, actually. Whenever he was in the same room as the man, Brody found his eyes automatically tracking to Lark. He drank the man in like a camel after a ten-day desert trek. Lark's energy and vitality drew him in. The way he moved. The way he was almost always laughing and smiling. The way he sometimes sought Zak out just to share a moment—a look, a word or a brief touch.

Suddenly, the memory of Zak's big calloused hand, resting and caressing against the back of his neck, sent a shiver of need down Brody's spine. It had been so good. He fully admitted he had let himself indulge and enjoy the touch for a moment. Such strong hands.

The thought of Zak throwing him down and taking him had nearly had Brody coming right then and there.

Glancing up to make sure Zak hadn't noticed was the worst mistake he could ever have made. For those first few, powerful seconds, they had connected. It was obvious, to both of them how attracted they were to each other, and just as obvious that it couldn't come to anything. The shuttered, closed off look that had replaced Zak's long, hot stare had almost brought Brody to his knees.

But he was right. They needed some distance, needed to keep things cool and professional. Zak had a good thing going with Lark. More than a good thing. It was precious. Brody couldn't come between that. He refused to come between them. He just wouldn't.

With a slightly sick sense of apprehension, Brody got back to his prep work.

Please, just let it all work out okay.

Chapter Four

Lark had never been so glad to get to the end of a Saturday night close. It had been a hell of a shift—busy, noisy and with enough back-to-back bookings to keep them all hopping. But the restaurant wasn't to blame for the current knot of tension settling in between his shoulder blades and cruising up to cramp his neck muscles. That special honour resided solely with two very stubborn, suspiciously absent men.

Pushing the menus back into their pigeonhole below the front desk, Lark looked around the now peaceful room. The wait-staff were milling around, finishing off the last of their jobs. Rio and Gus were chatting with the barman, and Dave and Andy had just pushed through the kitchen door, heading straight for their favourite little waitress, Jaime. It was time to make his move.

Lark strode through the dim restaurant—head held high, determination etched into every step as he made his way towards the kitchen. He wasn't too proud to admit he couldn't take it anymore. He'd tried to be accommodating and wait for Zak and Brody to stop dancing around one another. He'd truly wanted to let the men get over whatever it was that was bothering them about the situation—making them hesitate and edge around one another for weeks. But he'd run out of patience now. Nothing was happening, and he was going out of his mind watching Zak become more silent and stoic while Brody got more nervous and jittery.

Actually, Lark was rather surprised he'd lasted this long. They'd been around each other two weeks now. The hormone overload alone was threatening to send him over the edge. But neither Zak nor Brody seemed willing to admit to the scorching attraction between them. It was hot watching them eye each other—the long, lustful looks, the heat that rose in both men's cheeks when they were caught looking—but it was time to call it.

So now Lark was on a mission. Or maybe a hunt might be a more appropriate analogy. Whatever it was, he'd run out of patience with the ambiguity and self-doubt, longing looks and frustrating hesitations. He was moving on to the fun stuff, even if he had to drag both men kicking and screaming.

Okay, that might be a slight exaggeration. Not to mention a ridiculous impossibility. Lark didn't think he'd be able to drag either man very far against his will, especially since Lark probably didn't weight much more than Zak's left leg. But he was getting to work on sorting out just where everyone stood and what they all wanted. Because the three of them fighting their growing desire for each other just wasn't the way Lark wanted to expend his energy. He had much more...creative ideas about what they could be doing.

If I can just get the other two to stop hiding from this!

Of course, it would help if he could find Brody right now. The sweet little kitchen hand haunted his dreams with his piercing pale blue eyes, tall lean frame and absolutely gorgeous, unruly mane of dark blond hair, but he certainly didn't haunt the restaurant. He could be found there only when on duty. And Brody's shift was over, so if Lark didn't track him down soon, Brody was likely to slip out the door again right under his nose.

He was frustratingly good at that. And with the busy Saturday night trade done for the week, it only left tonight and tomorrow to figure something out. Otherwise, another three whole days would pass before Lark could get a chance to corner him about this. And Lark couldn't stand the thought of waiting that long.

Unfortunately, even after tackling Brody, he'd still have to work on Zak—which was going to be a completely different battle altogether. Lark knew Zak was attracted to Brody every bit as much as he was. The man could hardly keep his eyes off the luscious, sex-on-a-stick dishwasher. Zak just refused to admit it. And every time Lark had tried to talk about Brody, Zak had changed the subject or found something urgent that needed doing somewhere else. Infuriating man!

It was quite astonishing, really, to think of Zak—the normally staid and sensible man he loved—being as taken with Brody as he was. Zak wasn't the sort to have a roving eye. It wasn't in his makeup. Lark, on the other hand, took every opportunity he could get to appreciate a fine looking man.

In fact, he thought that Zak's inability to stop looking at Brody was a good sign that this was something that was meant to be. They were meant to explore this unexpected situation.

Lark was a bit vague on the whole coincidence versus destiny thing, but he did know that this felt right. So he was going for it.

Lark made his way to the office and breathed a sigh of relief when he caught sight of Brody. Thank goodness. The man he'd set his sights on hadn't somehow managed to give him the slip this time.

Actually, it was more a stifled moan of appreciation than a sigh of relief, Lark was forced to admit as he watched Brody standing by the small row of lockers along the office's far wall. Head bent, hands on his hips, looking down at his feet—he was stunning. Like one of those hunky men they posed shirtless in the cowboy calendars. All he needed was the battered hat tilted casually over his eyes and the boots. Oh! And one of those coy smiles Lark always found himself drooling over. Actually, Brody would look amazing wearing one of those smiles—and nothing else.

Brody dropped to one knee to fiddle with his laces. Lark couldn't help but imagine what else the man might be able to accomplish in that position.

* * * *

Brody was absolutely exhausted. Every muscle ached; and if he never saw another soap bubble or dirty pan again, he'd be a very happy man. Unfortunately, he would have to come back and do it all again tomorrow.

Paycheque, Brody. Paycheque, he reminded himself sternly, hating the fact he was whining about being stiff and sore when only a couple of weeks ago he'd been desperate enough to start thinking about turning tricks in some dark alley somewhere just to keep a roof over their heads.

Looking down, he noticed that one of his bootlaces had come undone. For a second, he considered leaving it. It really did seem like too much effort to bend down and retie it at the moment. But on second thought, the last thing he needed was to trip over it and break something. It would be hard to earn a paycheque with a broken arm, especially since he spent most of his shift elbows-deep in hot water.

Groaning, he dropped down and started working on the ratty laces. After he finished, he took a few extra seconds to try and find enough energy and enthusiasm to stand back up again. It wasn't easy.

"Are you okay?" Lark asked from the doorway, startling Brody enough that he bounced right back up to stand – and banged his arm painfully on his open locker door.

Ah, shit! That hurt! He'd nearly done himself exactly the sort of serious injury he'd been trying to avoid. Fucking shoelaces.

Jumping up like that was a stupid thing to do, but Brody really wanted to hide his exhaustion. He didn't want his boss thinking he was weak or some sort of pathetic loser that couldn't even hack the first few weeks in a new job.

Lark crossed the room with a slight frown of worry on his face and reached out to touch his arm.

Brody nearly moaned when he felt Lark's small hand caress his forearm, stroking over the light covering of hairs there and sending warmth coursing through him.

Even after two weeks Brody was still having a disturbingly powerful reaction to the man. At first he thought it was because he hadn't had sex in what felt like forever. Now he wasn't so sure.

Just when Brody had almost managed to get his reaction under control enough to start speaking without embarrassing himself, Zak walked into the room. Brody could have cursed in frustration. Were they trying to kill him here? What was it about these two men that got him all hot and bothered and sent blood pumping straight to his overeager cock every time? He couldn't be in the same room with the two of them without popping wood. It was an eternal source of embarrassment and a constant worry that they would figure him out and toss him out the door — probably with Zak's extra large boot mark on his ass.

Zak frowned at him, and Brody's thoughts turned to how it must look — with Lark standing so close and touching him. He took a hasty step back away from Lark, afraid the bigger man was about to take issue with the contact.

"Hey! Brody are you all right?" Zak asked.

He was concerned about me, not what we were doing? Fuck, this is making me crazy!

Brody was glad he hadn't made an idiot of himself trying to explain the innocence of Lark's actions. It wasn't as if he could claim the same innocent feelings towards either man, but he didn't ever want them to figure that out.

Brody answered Zak's question by nodding his head absently. He didn't trust his voice right now. And he was making enough of an idiot of himself already. Why would Zak feel threatened by him anyway? There was just no comparison between the two of them. The man was gorgeous. A walking sex god! No way would Brody ever be a threat to him physically for Lark's affection. And he had seen the way Lark looked at his lover, too. He adored Zak. They shared heated glances and long, loving stares all the time.

Suddenly, Brody had to get out. He wasn't ready to analyse the way he was feeling right now, but he was pretty certain it had a lot to do with that nasty little green eyed monster called jealousy. Trouble was he wasn't sure who he was more jealous of, Zak or Lark. He had the sinking feeling it might be both. Either way, he hated the feeling. He liked Lark and Zak. They were good people. Nice. Generous. Sexy…Fuck!

"You sure you're okay?" Lark asked, still looking worried.

"I…ahh…I'm fine," Brody stammered, stepping away from both men, not quite able to meet their eyes. "I-I have to go. I'll see you both tomorrow."

"Brody—" Lark started to call out to him, but Zak cut him off.

"Okay, Brody. We'll see you tomorrow."

Brody didn't hang around long enough to hear what Lark said to Zak. He hustled out of the room. He really wasn't ready to hear the two of them talking about him—questioning his strange behaviour, wondering if he was going to be able to keep up and do the job. Brody was determined that he would. He just had to prove it to everyone, including himself. That and get his unruly cock under control!

As he pushed his way through the kitchen doors, Brody saw the rest of the staff collecting their stuff and filing out the door under Rio's watchful eyes. Brody shook his head. The man acted like a prison warder. And wasn't that just a blast from the past.

"Come on, Brody," Rio commanded.

An impatient prison warder.

As Brody trudged wearily over to follow the others out, he compulsively checked his coat pocket for his wallet. He felt his heart stutter in his chest when his hand met only the cool, smooth, and empty lining of his jacket.

Oh, shit! I have to go back. He must have been so preoccupied with making sure Lark and Zak didn't notice his hard-on as he got away from them as fast as possible, that he hadn't heard his wallet fall out somewhere between the kitchen office and the front door.

Brody froze in his tracks. There was no way he was going anywhere without his wallet.

"Come on, Brody!" Rio called tersely, still holding the door open to let everyone out.

"I must have dropped my wallet. I'm just going back to find it," Brody replied. He continued to rummage through his pockets, just in case he had put it somewhere else, but he knew he hadn't. He was always extremely careful about where he put his wallet.

Rio frowned as if preparing to argue with him when Gus started grumbling.

"Just let him go back, Rio. Zak and Lark are still in there somewhere. Come on man, I just want to get out of here, and since I brought your scrawny ass in, I guess I have to drop it back off home, too."

Rio hesitated for a moment, but finally relented.

"Make sure you pull the door closed properly behind you. It's self-locking, but test it too," Rio reminded him.

Brody managed not to roll his eyes at the uptight head chef. *I know how to close a fucking door!* But it wouldn't do to upset the man. While Zak and Lark were technically his bosses, in a kitchen, no one mouthed off to the head chef and lived to tell the tale.

Besides, he really was more worried about his wallet—the wallet that now had fifty bucks in it thanks to being paid a few days ago. Fifty bucks he needed to buy Wolf some more medicine. He didn't have enough energy to waste worrying about the head chef's obsessive-compulsive power trips.

Turning around as Rio pulled the door firmly shut, Brody began to search the floor. He carefully retraced his steps back through the restaurant and into the kitchen. He was at the office door before he knew it, and he was really starting to panic. He couldn't afford to lose fifty bucks.

Then he heard it. A low moan followed by an unmistakable grunt of male pleasure. Brody froze at the slightly ajar office door, unable to go forward, but unable to turn away either.

He could see the warm yellow light from the desk lamp spilling out over the hard kitchen tiles at his feet and was drawn almost against his will to nudge the door so he could see inside. Once he did, he couldn't tear his eyes away from the sight in front of him, no matter how much he knew he should turn and walk away and pretend he'd never been there.

Lark knelt in front of Zak, his head bobbing back and forth over Zak's long, hard cock as he sucked and licked at it over and over again. Both their eyes were closed in bliss, and as Brody watched, Zak brought a big, square hand up to the side of Lark's head and gently caressed the soft, golden blond strands of his hair.

He heard Lark's soft murmur of delight and saw Zak's hips rock forward into his mouth. Zak obviously enjoyed the sensation of Lark's vocalization and tongue across his hard shaft.

"Oh, Lark! So good," Zak groaned.

The murmured praise seemed to spur Lark on. His cheeks hollowed with renewed vigour and his pace sped up. Brody could hear the smaller man making soft mewling noises around the thick shaft in his mouth and had to bite into his lower lip to stifle a groan. He knew he should look away, realised that he was spying on an incredibly intimate moment he had no right to see, but he couldn't seem to stop watching them.

When Lark reached down with one hand to free his own cock, then began to jerk its long thin length in time with his rhythmic sucking, Brody was lost. He couldn't have looked away to save his life. Adjusting himself, he pressed his hand firmly against his hard-on, relieving some of the ache in his rapidly swelling cock.

As he watched, Lark reached up with his free hand and began to caress and manipulate Zak's full, heavy balls. Zak's hips thrust forward again, only this time he seemed powerless to halt them. He continued to thrust in and out of Lark's mouth—no longer caressing Lark's hair, but holding his lover's head firmly in place so he could fuck the smaller man's face. Lark's moans only increased in intensity and the hand on his cock sped up.

"Oh, Fuck, Lark! Coming, baby. Coming!"

With that, Zak gave one last lunging thrust into Lark's mouth and cried out his release. Brody watched as Lark swallowed Zak's seed down in deep, desperate gulps while Lark's cock exploded over the floor between them in long streams of pearly white cum.

When Zak opened his eyes to look down at Lark, who still knelt at his feet, Brody stumbled back, terrified of being caught and mortified that he had watched the private moment between the lovers. He tried to turn around to make a break for it, but his clumsy, hurried movements sent him crashing into a mobile workbench. Before he could regain his feet, Zak's sharp call stopped Brody in his tracks. Brody knew what he'd done was very wrong, and he desperately wanted to run away and hide, but doing so would be the ultimate in cowardice. And he refused to be thought of as a coward.

"Brody!" Zak shouted again as he stepped out of the office, his hands still finishing the last of the buttons on his fly.

Lark hovered at his side, nervously looking back and forth between them.

"I'm sorry...I didn't mean to—"

"It's okay, Brody," Lark said softly.

Lark reached up to stroked Zak's chest soothingly with his small, pale hand then stretched his hand out to Brody. For a second, Brody had the distinct impression Lark was trying to include him, almost like the smaller man really wanted him to be there. But then Lark hesitated, as if unsure of how the gesture would be received.

"Are you all right?" Zak asked in a low, serious rumble.

"I...ah...sure. I mean..." Brody struggled as he tried to get the right words marshalled together and out of his mouth without making a fool of himself. "Yeah, I'm...fine...I just...I just lost my wallet."

"Oh!" Lark cried, stepping back into the office and beginning to search the floor while Brody and Zak continued to stare at each other. "Let's see...it probably just fell out..."

As Lark continued to babble behind them like a happy little brook while he searched, the silence between Brody and Zak stretched out. Looking into Zak's intense changeable green-brown eyes before lingering over the shadow of stubble on his cheeks, Brody found himself wanting to reach out to run his hand down the side of the man's face. He wanted to feel the coarseness of it against his fingers.

"Ah! Found it," Lark cried in triumph. He returned holding up Brody's battered wallet.

Brody reached to take it from Lark's hands, being careful not to actually touch him. He tried not to remember watching him caressing Zak's thighs. Or seeing him hold Zak's hips while his mouth worked at his lover's cock. Or the desperate desire Brody had felt to join them. To have Lark's mouth and hands on him. To share a kiss that would keep Zak's mouth just as occupied.

"I…um…thanks," Brody murmured, not sure what to do now. His body wanted him to step forward, wrap his arms around Lark and lean into Zak. His mind was in complete chaos and no help at all. His sense of self-preservation was telling him to run. And all the while, his cock was demanding to know what the hell the holdup was!

"I'll walk you out and lock up behind you," Zak suggested, breaking the awkward silence.

"Zak—" Lark began, but Zak cut him off again.

"I'll be back in a minute, Lark. Just…I won't be long."

Zak strode away and Brody had no choice but to trail along after him. With one last glance at Lark, who mouthed 'it'll be okay', Brody followed Zak out.

As Zak held open the front door, Brody paused and looked up into the bigger man's eyes.

"I'm sorry. I—"

"It's okay, Brody. We'll see you tomorrow," Zak said solemnly.

"Wait!" Lark called out as he hurried towards them.

"Lark..." Zak warned, but Lark waved him off and stepped up to put a hand on Brody's arm.

"It really is okay, Brody."

Lark's eyes where more serious than Brody had ever seen them in the short time he'd known the man.

"I'm really sorry for intruding," Brody whispered sincerely.

"That's okay. In fact...I wish I'd have known you were there. That would have been hot."

Brody just stared, too stunned to say anything. He couldn't believe he wasn't being fired. The idea that Lark thought his spying had been hot was...well, hot.

"Come on, Lark," Zak said gently, drawing the smaller man away. "Let the man get home. It's been a long night."

Impulsively, Lark pulled away from Zak and kissed Brody lightly on the cheek.

"Think about it," he whispered softly into Brody's ear before stepping away.

Brody looked up sharply at Zak, but he wasn't sure the man had heard. Zak was just watching him. Not angry, but not encouraging either.

Confusing thoughts and desires spinning around in his head, Brody walked out the door and onto the footpath. The door closed quietly behind him. After he heard the lock turn, he couldn't help but look back and watch the two men—Zak's arm slung casually over Lark's shoulders—as they navigated their way through the tables and back to the kitchen again.

Brody shook his head. He wasn't sure what had just happened, but he was pretty certain it was going to keep him up long into the morning when he should be

Jade Archer

sleeping. And that would be after dealing with the
unruly cock that threatened to break his zipper with
its insistence that he go back in, grab Lark for a proper
kiss, and beg Zak to fuck him.

* * * *

Lark wrapped his arms around Zak's waist and
leaned into his poor lover.

Zak stood in the middle of the office—hands on his
hips and a slight frown on his face—as if not quite
sure what to do with himself.

Lark knew it had probably been the right thing to
do, letting Brody go, giving him some space to think
things through. But he didn't have to like it. And it
didn't look like Zak was too keen on the idea either.

"He's cute," Lark whispered into Zak's chest,
hoping to get his reticent lover to talk about what had
just happened.

Giving them some space and time to think things
through didn't mean Lark was going to let either man
avoid the issue or dictate the pace on whatever it was
that was happening between them anymore. While he
didn't know Brody very well—yet—it had become
increasingly obvious the man wouldn't be breaking
any land speed records getting them together. And
Lark knew if it were left to Zak, they'd still be dancing
round each other well into their nineties. And that just
wasn't acceptable.

"Who?" Zak said evasively, stiffening up and
betraying himself even as he tried to plead ignorance.

Lark looked up at him. There was no way they were
going to play these sorts of games. Not after the scene
that had just played out between the three of them.
Lark was determined to pull it all out into the open

right here and now. He had no intention of letting Zak avoid the conversation this time.

"Don't, Lark," Zak warned, pulling away from him before Lark could utter a word.

Damn! The man knew him to well.

Zak strode over to the desk and pretended to look through the mess of paperwork scattered across its scarred surface.

"I've seen how you watch him, you know," Lark said casually as he watched Zak's every tense move.

"What are you talking about?"

Once again Lark stared across at his lover and quirked an eyebrow. He knew he didn't have to tell Zak he was full of shit. The man would know just by 'the look'.

"Okay. So he's good looking. That doesn't mean anything." Zak replied defensively as he spun around to face Lark again, the paperwork completely forgotten once more.

"Zak! He's gorgeous! And I know you've noticed."

"We've had this conversation before, Lark. You do it all the time, but it's just looking. Window shopping." Zak was silent for a moment, and Lark could see him fighting through something in his head. The expression of sadness and confusion on Zak's face was painful to see. It was so unlike him to flounder like this.

Lark wanted to reach out, wrap Zak up in his arms and help him through whatever it was that bothered him so much about the situation. But he forced himself to wait. Zak needed to work through it himself.

"I'd never cheat on you, Lark. Never," Zak finally said in a shaky whisper.

"It's not exactly cheating if I know about it, Zak," Lark replied softly.

Zak studied him for a moment and Lark held his breath, wondering what was going through his lover's mind right now. For the first time in a very long while, he really had no idea. This was so far outside any of their experiences, either together or apart, that he didn't know what to expect. He simply had to wait and see. And hope.

"I've seen the way you look at him too," Zak accused without any heat.

Lark shrugged. "So we both think he's gorgeous. You aren't the only one in the family with good taste, you know."

"Is this your way of telling me you want to fuck him?" Zak demanded, tension and anxiety radiating from every line of his stiff body. "Is that it, Lark? Are you...?" Zak swallowed and looked away.

"No! It's not like that. I'd never cheat on you either."

"Then what are you saying?"

"I just think—"

"Are you bored with me, Lark? Is that it? Are you looking for someone new because I'm not what you want anymore? Is that what all this sudden interest in toys and other men is all about?" Zak's voice was tight and so strained it ended on a whisper, as if it had been forced out of a throat that desperately wanted to close up and hold the possibility in.

"What?! No!" Lark cried, rushing forward to wrap his arms around Zak again. Pressing close, Lark heard Zak's heart pounding and felt his own pulse racing with dread at the thought of losing this man. His soul mate. "I'm not bored with you, Zak. Never that. I don't want to lose you! It doesn't have to be like that. I just...I just think we should explore this thing a bit."

"So you are bored!"

"No!" This time it was Lark's turn to pull away and run his hands through his hair in frustration. "I can't explain it, Zak. I just can't help feeling there's something we're missing."

"Missing?" Zak demanded incredulously, the hurt in his voice raw and stark.

Shit! I'm screwing this all up so badly. And it's hurting Zak! And that was the very last thing Lark ever wanted to do. If he could just work out some way to explain what he was feeling. All he wanted was for Zak to understand. But he didn't seem to be able to get the words out right.

"Not 'missing', as in not enough. 'Missing', as in there's more!" Lark sighed in frustration. "I just think you should…you know. Seduce him."

"What?" Zak shouted, his hands going to his hips as he went from hurt to outrage in the blink of an eye.

Oops, that hadn't come out right, either.

"I think he's into you, Zak. I just—"

"Are you fucking crazy? The man just caught you sucking my cock! I hardly think he's going to be lining up to do the same!"

"I wouldn't be so sure about that."

"Brody is not a cock whore, Lark," Zak growled at him.

"What!" *Where the hell did that come from?* "I never said he was, Zak. And are you saying I am?" he demanded, feeling his hackles rise.

"No! That's not what I said, and you know it. Brody's not…he just…he's not some casual fling."

Lark stopped and took the time to really study Zak for a moment. Every muscle was rigid and his jaw was so tense, Lark was afraid the man might crack a tooth if he didn't ease up soon. The longer Lark looked, the more obvious it became that Zak wasn't just fighting the attraction because he didn't want to upset their relationship and possibly hurt Lark, but because he didn't think it could go anywhere. He didn't want to use or hurt Brody either. Apparently, Zak was a whole lot more attached and emotionally involved with Brody than Lark had given him credit for.

"I never suggested he was just a fling, Zak," Lark said carefully, watching Zak attentively the whole time. "I just said I think he's really interested in you."

"What are you talking about?"

"He was holding that jacket in front of him pretty damn protectively, like a shield. And I saw the way he was looking at you when I came back with the wallet. He was more than just a bit embarrassed. I'd say he was all but begging you to let him suck you off."

"You're delusional!"

Lark took a deep breath and tried for patience. What he really wanted to do was grab Zak by his bulging biceps and shake the stuffing out of him. Unfortunately, owing to the considerable size difference between them, that wasn't going to be possible. So he tried a different approach—being reasonable.

"I love you, Zak. I don't want to lose you, but there's something more for us. I know there is. I don't know what it is, but I won't pretend the need isn't there. I can't lose us, Zak. Not if all it takes is for us to be brave enough to try something different. And I won't back away from this, either. It's too important. I know it is. I can feel it."

For a long time, he wasn't sure Zak was going to acknowledge what he'd said. How he felt. But then gradually the tension melted from Zak's muscles and face, and Zak nodded slowly.

"I know you'd never back down, baby. Not if it's something you really feel is important. You're one of the bravest men I know. And you won't lose me. We won't lose us. I promise." Zak opened his arms and Lark stepped into the warm, welcoming embrace that meant home, just as it always had. "It's not like it'll be the first time you slapped me around until I saw sense. Assuming this *is* actually going to make sense sometime soon..."

Lark choked on a laugh. For a long time they stood together, holding each other and letting their embrace dissipate the fear and worry. Slowly, Lark felt the two of them relax into one another, and he knew everything would be all right between them.

"Zak?" he whispered quietly.

"Yes, sweetheart?"

"I like him too. I just thought...if you... then we could both maybe..."

Zak sighed and pulled him a little closer. "Honestly, I'll be surprised if we see him again. I think...I don't know, Lark. There's just something...lost and vulnerable about Brody. We may have scared him off. And I'm not saying that's necessarily a bad thing."

"But if we do—see him again I mean—do you think..."

"Lark. I don't want to push him...Brody...I think Brody needs us to give him space and time. He doesn't need us to jump on him and try to whisk him off to our bed."

"But that sounds like so much fun," Lark protested with a cheeky little pouting smile. For once Zak didn't join in his playfulness.

"Brody's not a plaything, Lark. He's not some new toy you get to unwrap and experiment with. If you want to do this then you have to promise me it's not just because you want something new to play with. I won't toy with Brody."

Lark pulled away a little to look up into Zak's determined face. It gave him pause for a moment. Something more was going on. He could feel it in the tense muscles under his fingers and the way Zak clenched his jaw again at the mention of treating Brody with anything but the utmost care and respect.

Maybe Zak was a lot closer to coming to the same conclusion about Brody than Lark had thought.

Lark was already well and truly convinced that Brody was someone they were meant to meet and get to know more intimately. He'd just never expected his normally obsessively cautious and methodical lover to get to the same point so quickly. He'd thought that by slowly introducing the idea of letting Brody into their bed, he might have some hope of getting Zak to see Brody in their everyday lives as well. But apparently Zak's heart was leading the way.

Lark felt a kernel of hope grow inside him.

But for now, he decided to back off. Whatever was happening was subtle and fragile and he didn't want to push it right now.

"It's not that at all, Zak. I don't see Brody as a new toy to play with, I promise."

Zak studied him for a long time and Lark held his eyes steadfastly, not looking away for a moment. He had to make Zak see how very serious he was about his last words. Lark couldn't explain it, exactly, but he knew that this was more important to him — to them — than a game or play time. That Brody mattered to them. That this was going to be one of the most important moments of their lives.

Finally, Zak simply nodded. Whatever he had been looking for in Lark's eyes, he had obviously found.

Zak's shoulders relaxed and his voice returned to its normal, calm cadence.

Lark sighed in relief at having past the impromptu test.

"Let's go home."

Lark nodded, suddenly more tired than he could ever remember being. He just wanted to cuddle up in bed with Zak and sleep for a week. It had been a long, frustrating few days, and it didn't look like there was going to be any quick, easy answers anytime soon. But as much as sleep called to him, he knew it would be a long time coming. His brain was already playing this evening over and over in his mind, and a certain wide-eyed, hunky kitchen-hand took centre stage. It was just a pity he'd exited stage left. Lark wouldn't mind cuddling up against Brody, too.

Chapter Five

Brody hefted the heavy bag of groceries he held in one hand and tightened his grip on the little chemist's bag he clutched in the other. He knew he was being paranoid, but consciously feeling the weight of the medicine in his hand reassured him. He didn't want Wolf to go without, but if he accidently lost the little bag and its expensive contents he wouldn't be able to replace it. At least, not this month.

Happy that he had everything well in hand, he turned to begin the long trek back to the apartment when he heard someone calling out his name.

"Brody! Hey, Brody!"

Lark.

Brody closed his eyes. He'd lain awake half the night worrying about what he was going to say, and he still didn't know.

Fuck! He wasn't ready for this. He'd thought he had at least a few more hours to sort out the confusing mess from last night and come up with something before he had to face Lark and Zak again. Now, as he

68

stood frozen to the spot, the small bag of Wolf's medicine dangling from one hand and a heavy bag of groceries in the other, he felt like the proverbial deer caught in the headlights.

He couldn't seem to wrap his head around his intense, needy reaction to Zak and Lark. And discovering that they might actually welcome his attraction only added to his confusion.

Still, as Lark raced up—his sweet, infectious smile lighting up his face—Brody couldn't help but be glad to see him. His heart rate ratcheted up another few notches and his breath hitched at how hot the man was, and how truly pleased he seemed to be to see Brody. It warmed Brody right through, even as he tried frantically to think of a way to get away without seeming rude.

I'm such a mess. And confusion wasn't the worst of it. Somewhere deep down, in a part of himself he tried desperately to deny, Brody was pretty sure he could fall hard and fast for this beautiful man and his gorgeous lover.

"Hi, Brody! How are things going?"

"Fine," was all Brody managed to get out without tripping over his tongue as he took in Lark's tight pants and plain white shirt that moulded to his small but well-defined chest.

Well, that was good, he thought sarcastically. So articulate, and now he was hard enough to pound nails. Thank goodness he'd put on his tightest jeans. At least there was some hope that Lark wouldn't notice his 'growing' problem. The painful constriction in his pants, however, was less of a blessing.

"Are you doing anything?" Lark asked brightly. "Maybe we could grab a coffee or something."

"Sorry. I...ah...I have to go. Got to get these things home before they spoil." Brody was quite pleased with the flash of brilliance that gave him a valid reason to scurry away like the silly little mouse he was. At least for a few more hours anyway. Hopefully, that would be enough to sort out what was going on in his head—the one on his shoulders that is. The one in his pants was far more decisive about what it wanted.

"Zak's just talking to a new supplier he wants to try out for the restaurant. We could run you home so you could put your shopping away and then all go out somewhere." Lark suggested hopefully.

"I'm sorry...I...ah...I really have to go." There was no way he wanted Lark to see where he was living. It might be reasonably clean and infinitely preferable to the streets, but it was still a dump compared to where Zak and Lark lived—above the restaurant, with its glorious views over the river passage and down to the ocean.

"I was really hoping we could talk about last night. Away from the restaurant where we'd have more time and less pressure," Lark persisted.

Brody shifted uncomfortably. He wasn't ready to talk yet. He still hadn't worked out what he felt, or what the two men's motivations might be.

"I'm sorry. Can it wait? I really—"

"Is there someone else? Is that it?" Lark asked, his usual light, happy voice now sombre and serious.

"No...I mean, yes. I have to get back to Wolf." He held up the chemist's bag as evidence that he wasn't just brushing Lark off—even though he was. "He's been sick."

"Wolf? Is that your boyfriend?" Lark asked in a flat, even tone that was a little scary coming from the normally bright and bubbly man.

"No!" Brody denied quickly. He didn't want Lark to think he wasn't interested or was messing them around. He just needed some time to think. "Wolf's my brother and I really need to get back and check on him...I'm not—I mean, I want to stay. I like you and Zak, but—"

"It's okay, Brody." Zak's voice interrupted from behind them. A large, warm hand settled on Brody's shoulder, surprising him and nearly making him fumble the precious bag of medicine. "Lark's just being his usual pushy self."

Stepping around to stand beside Lark, Zak looked down at the smaller blond man and reached out to squeeze his hand gently.

"There's no rush, is there, Lark? We'll try to catch up and hang out another day."

"But—"

"Lark, just leave it, baby. Give Brody some room. There's no rush." Zak grinned down at Lark, softening his reprimand with a tender look.

Lark nodded, even though he didn't look at all happy about the decision.

"But you know we could still give you a lift home. Those bags look heavy."

"No!" Brody blurted out too quickly. Zak's eyebrows shot up in surprise at his abrupt outburst. "I mean, it's really not that far and I don't want to put you out."

"It wouldn't put us out. We wouldn't mind at all. Would we, Zak?" Lark looked up at Zak expectantly, but the bigger, muscular man continued to focus intensely on Brody, assessing and measuring him carefully.

Brody flushed. He was pretty sure Zak knew he was too embarrassed to let them see where he lived. He could only imagine what he was thinking at the moment.

"If you're sure..." Zak said, still watching him closely.

"I'm sure. I...ah...I'll see you guys later. I better get home before Wolf misses me. He can be a bit of a tyrant when he's sick."

* * * *

As Zak watched Brody's firm ass, encased in the tightest pair of jeans he'd seen in a long time, hurry off down the street, he couldn't help but worry about the other man. Something wasn't right. He was so tempted to follow Brody and see what was going on.

But he couldn't. If Brody was ever going to trust them, they had to respect his privacy. Zak could wait until the man was ready to tell them his secrets.

Zak knew that Lark was disappointed because Brody wasn't opening up to them right now. He never had been very patient, and Zak knew Lark wanted to talk to Brody about what had happened last night. He probably wanted to suss Brody out, find out everything there was to know about the man and work out, in graphic detail, how they might all fit together.

Lark would definitely want to hurry them on to the next step. Then, more than likely, skip over several more steps to get to the good bits, as Lark was so fond of saying. But Zak was very conscious that it wasn't the way to go. Not with Brody. Not between the three of them. Whatever had gone on in Brody's life before, whatever was still going on, required some delicate handling and restraint.

"I don't like this, Zak. Something's wrong. Something's worrying Brody. And I don't think it's just what happened last night. It's something else," Lark said as he turned with a worried look on his face from watching the same tight, denim-covered ass walk away.

"Maybe he's not interested, Lark. He just might be too polite or worried about his job to say anything. Did you ever consider that?"

"Please," Lark drawled, rolling his eyes at him, "the man practically trips over his tongue whenever he sees you. Did you see him when you touched him just now? Whoa, baby, that was hot! No. He's interested. I know he is. But something's holding him back."

Zak suspected he was right, but he'd wanted to hear whether his lover thought so, too. It helped to know they were both on the same page. Although, Lark seemed to have missed the scorching hot stares Brody frequently threw his way, as well. He'd have to keep an eye on that. If things ever went any further—and right now that was far from certain—it was imperative that everyone feel equally wanted and desired.

"What should we do? Do you think he's in some sort of trouble? Should we go after him?" Lark asked, a frown creasing his usually happy face as he looked back down the street in the direction Brody had taken.

"No. Just leave it for now, sweetheart."

Lark definitely didn't look happy with the idea.

"Forcing him to tell you his private business isn't the way, Lark. Just give him some time."

While he still didn't look thrilled, Lark nodded his head in agreement, obviously seeing the sense in what

Zak had said. How long that might last, Zak wasn't sure. But he'd take what he could get of the smaller man's compliance while it lasted.

He gently turned Lark around and gave him a soft push to start him walking in the opposite direction. When Lark looked over his shoulder and poked his tongue out, Zak grinned, but remained determined to keep a tight rein on his impetuous lover. Brody required careful handling and time, more than anything else. Lark might not be naturally inclined to give it to him, but Zak was going to do his best to see that he got it.

Although he was hesitant to allow the natural attraction the three of them seemed to share develop, if it was inevitable—and it really looked like it was— Zak was going to see that it developed so both Brody and Lark were protected. There was no way he thought either man was out to hurt the other, but they were entering new and strange territory, and they were all going to have to tread with care.

"Come on, Lark. Let's go get that coffee."

Chapter Six

Brody felt tight and hyper-sensitised. The slightest movement, caught out of the corner of his eye when someone got too close, had him fumbling and dropping things, stumbling over his own feet in his haste to see who approached. Brody both dreaded and craved the moment when Zak or Lark—or both—would seek him out.

All worked up and anxious; Brody was a walking disaster area just waiting to happen. Fortunately, he hadn't actually broken anything, but he knew it was only a matter of time. This couldn't go on. Something had to give. The only trouble was Brody was pretty sure it was going to be his mind.

Finally, in frustration and disgust, Gus sent him out the back to clean the seals on the fridges and 'get his fucking head on straight' as the man so eloquently put it. Talk about the crappiest job Gus could possibly have come up with. It was obvious he had been saving it up for a special occasion when someone truly pissed him off. But to be honest, Brody was so relieved he could have kissed the irritable chef.

Then again, maybe not. But Brody did leave the kitchen with a spring in his step, grateful for the opportunity to get out and tuck himself away in the quiet storage area out the back. No one was likely to disturb him there. More to the point, Zak and Lark were hardly likely to find him. There was no real reason for them to venture back there, because the chefs did all the ordering and restocking.

It was just a pity no one mentioned the details of the plan to whatever higher powers were on duty that day. Either that or they had a very sick sense of humour. Because as Brody hurried around the shelving in the cool, dark room, stacked high with supplies and ingredients, he almost ran straight into the very two men he was so desperately trying to avoid.

Zak had Lark pinned against the wall and was leaning down into him, ravaging his mouth in a deep, passionate kiss.

"Oh, God! I'm sorry!" Brody stumbled backwards and tried to make a break for it. Not again!

"No! Brody! Wait!" Lark called after him.

For a moment Brody seriously considered ignoring him and running away as fast as his legs would go. But he knew he couldn't do it. Firstly, because it was Lark that was calling him, and secondly because Zak would see him being a complete pussy.

He took a deep breath and slowly turned around to face the other men.

For a moment, he just looked between them—Lark small and pale, with his light blond hair in artful disarray and his bright, mischievous blue eyes studying him intensely, and Zak, taller, broader, darker and completely focussed on him with those smouldering, pale green-brown eyes.

Brody felt trapped and yet at the same time so very tempted. The way they looked at him...he felt wanted and desirable and yearned to just give himself over to them.

"This is ridiculous," Lark said, closing the distance between them and reaching out to run his hand lightly over Brody's forearm.

His touch left a trail of goosebumps, and Brody had to fight damn hard to suppress an appreciative shiver.

"I like you, Brody. As in, I think you're the hottest thing I've seen since I first laid eyes on Zak. And Zak likes you. As in, he pops wood every time he sees you and all but drools in your presence."

"Lark!" Zak protested, but Lark ignored him.

"I think you like us, too," Lark whispered, his voice rough and husky as he reached down and very lightly ran his hand up Brody's hard shaft through increasingly tight trousers.

Brody's cock throbbed in response to the other man's touch, and he realised he was in danger of embarrassing himself by coming in his pants. Brody groaned softly at the delicious torture, unable to make himself pull away.

"Lark!" Zak repeated, this time stepping forward to intervene.

A spike of fear shot through Brody. Not that Lark would get him off, but that Zak would make Lark stop.

Before Zak could brush Lark's hand away, or Brody could think better of it, Brody reached down to cover Lark's hand with his own, pressing it against his cock and giving the caress just the right amount of pressure for him to thrust against.

"Please," Brody whimpered shamelessly. He closed his eyes to savour the sensation of Lark's ministrations to his sensitive, throbbing shaft.

After a few moments enjoying Lark's hand, Brody blinked open his eyes and looked straight into Zak's stunned face. He felt heat rush to his face in embarrassment. It had been so long since he had been with a lover. So long since he could afford to lower his guard enough to risk getting close to someone. Worrying about Wolf had taken up all of his time and energy. Now that they were finally safe from the constant sex, drugs, and crime that had been their daily nightmare for the past four years, his cock seemed to have awoken with a vengeance.

Brody couldn't remember ever getting this hard before. It left him aching with need. A need he could afford to indulge for the first time since he had started his desperate bid to rescue his brother. But what must these men think of him at the moment? He was all but throwing himself at them like a common street whore.

Brody was just about to step away when he felt a soft touch to his cheek.

"Beautiful," Lark whispered as he gazed up at him with awe and desire in his eyes.

Brody didn't know what to say. When he sensed Zak move, he switched his gaze back to the bigger man. But instead of finding jealousy or anger in Zak's face, Brody saw that his eyes had gone molten with lust.

Lark began to rub his hand against Brody's cock again, breaking him out of his stupor. But all he could seem to utter was another lustful moan as his hips thrust forward completely of their own volition.

Apparently taking his groan of appreciation for consent, Lark reached to unfasten his pants. His movements were hurried and fumbling, as if he were nearly frantic with desire or expecting to be stopped at any moment.

"Lark!" Zak barked sharply, and this time Lark stilled. The tone of Zak's voice allowed no argument this time.

Both Lark and Brody froze, but Brody's cock twitched as Zak's commanding figure moved to hover over them.

"Zak—" Lark began to beg pitifully, but Zak cut him off with a stern look.

"If you have any doubts about this, Brody. If this isn't what you want, or even if it is, but you need more time, you need to say something now. No regrets. No taking it back."

Zak's uncompromising gaze held Brody transfixed. He wasn't sure what 'it' was, but he couldn't deny he wanted the two men. He wanted them so bad, his cock was about to have a permanent zipper imprint if it wasn't released soon. But he was equally unsure whether letting this continue wouldn't be one of the stupidest things he had ever done. It was just a pity all the blood was currently pooling in his groin, leaving only a skeleton crew on duty in his brain where he might have had some chance to make a sensible decision and veto the 'let's get it on' party in his pants.

Lark raised himself up on his tiptoes and planted a light, almost chaste kiss to Brody's cheek. "Whatever you decide, Brody. Really. There's no rush."

The sincerity and gentle regard, along with the certainty of how hard it had been for Lark—the fiery little go-getter—to say the words, did strange things to Brody in the region of his chest that he wasn't quite ready to face. He couldn't stop himself from tilting his head down to lightly kiss Lark's soft, pink lips.

He wouldn't regret this, whatever happened, wherever it might lead them. He wanted them. Needed them. And they wanted him. In the end, it was that simple.

When Lark kissed him back, Brody very tentatively ran the tip of his tongue over the other man's lips and was amazed when Lark opened to him immediately — sucking him in so their tongues tangled together. Pulling away, Brody thrilled when their lips clung together for a moment, as if their bodies didn't want to be parted. He stared down into Lark's heated eyes.

"I want this," Brody said, surprised when his voice came out low and steady. Turning his head, Brody looked straight into Zak's eyes so there would be no misunderstanding. "I want you both."

"Show me," Zak demanded in a gravel-rough rumble that made Brody shiver with lust.

"Shall we give Zak a show?" Lark asked, returning to the removal of Brody's pants with a cheeky smile on his face.

"As long as it's a hands-on demonstration," Brody replied. If this was the start of an affair between the three of them, he had no intention of being simply taken along for the ride. His days of being just pretty scenery and a tight hole to fuck were long, long over.

"I could come at that," Zak said, reaching down to adjust himself.

"Oh, Love!" Lark giggled. "That was terrible." He finally freed Brody's cock and began stroking it in long, smooth strokes.

Brody felt another pang in his chest. Oh, God! He was pathetic. Just hearing Lark say the word 'love' made him harder and so desperate, yet at the same time desolate and jealous. He wanted that, he realised with a shock. He wanted —

Brody shut the thought away with a loud mental clang, sealing it away from his conscious mind. He wouldn't think about it yet. Not now. Maybe not ever. In this moment, he would think only of Zak and Lark—two of the hottest men he had ever seen in his life, and they wanted him. Even if only for now.

"Open his pants," Lark whispered, breaking into Brody's chaotic thoughts.

"Huh?" Brody grunted.

Lark stroked him expertly, massaging and manipulating him so that it was difficult to process Lark's words.

"Zak looks uncomfortable. Open his pants for him. You wouldn't want him to hurt himself, would you?" Lark's eyes glittered with amusement.

Brody's gaze tracked to the huge erection distorting the front of Zak's trousers. It did look pretty painful all wrapped up like that. And so tempting.

Reaching across, Brody very carefully slipped the waist buttons free, but before he could lower the zipper, Zak took care of it himself. Brody understood why when Zak's long, thick shaft immediately sprang free and slapped into his hand with a soft, velvety bounce. Zak went commando.

Brody wrapped his hand around Zak's cock and began a slow exploration of the man's responses as he glided his fist up and down, varying the speed and intensity of his grip. When he rubbed his thumb over Zak's slit then slipped it down to run under the sensitive, hard head, Zak shuddered and gasped.

"Oh, yeah! Right there, baby."

Brody's pulse jumped at the small praise. He did it again and was delighted when he got an equally enthusiastic response.

"Come here," Zak growled, his eyes filled with desire as he reached out and wrapped his huge hand around the back of Brody's neck and pulled him in for a rough, passionate kiss. The man left no inch of his mouth unexplored by his thorough, questing tongue.

Brody hardly noticed that Lark had stopped stroking him until he felt a scorching, soft, wet caress across the head of his cock. He gasped and broke the kiss with Zak to stare down between their bodies. Lark knelt between them, a small fist wrapped around each cock, his hot, pink tongue bathing and licking around the heads.

"Lark!" Brody gasped, frantically fighting down the urge to come.

Lark looked up at him with an impish grin — it was obvious he knew exactly what he was doing to Brody. Lark's tongue swiped across his slit again before turning to Zak and doing the same thing to his lover.

To their lover, Brody correct.

For long minutes Lark alternated between them, first sucking and licking Zak's long, heavily veined shaft, then returning to lavish an equal amount of attention on Brody's. On and on Lark played with them — working them up to a fever point of need before offering lighter, gentler flicks of his tongue so they could regain control. But when Lark began to caress and manipulate Brody's balls, he couldn't take it anymore.

"Please!" Brody said, too far gone to feel embarrassed by the desperate whine in his voice.

Before Brody could truly work out what he wanted or from whom, Lark surged to his feet and opened his own trousers. The smaller man's cock was long and slender and felt like it burned into him as it came to rest against Brody's own hard shaft. Lark pressed his groin into Brody's and wrapped his hand around both their cocks, holding them up against their bellies. Then he began to pump them together.

"Ahh...oh...La...Lark...so..." Brody's praise was lost in the dizzying climb to ecstasy.

He felt Zak's broader hand push their shirts roughly up out of the way then wrap around them, taking over from Lark and completely engulfing their cocks in perfect pressure and friction. Zak tongued Brody with small, wet swipes at the sensitive spot just below his ear, and Brody thrust up into Zak's hand, tossing his head back in the final throes of their delicious euphoria.

"Come for me," Zak rasped.

As Zak leaned into him, Brody could feel that Zak had his own cock well in hand and was jerking himself off at the same time. With that thought, Brody exploded in a burst of white-hot pleasure. His shaft shot long bursts of seed that splashed up between them. The spray from Lark's cock bathed his belly an instant later, then Zak, too, shuddered against him.

Zak caught what he could in his hands and continued to pump and milk them all until he had coaxed out the very last drops. Then he put both his dripping hands together, mixing all their cum, and drew them back apart to look into his palms. As if he couldn't believe what he held there.

Lark dropped to his knees to lick their combined cum from Zak's hand. Zak stared at Brody, raising a questioning eyebrow as he raised his other hand and began to lick. Brody leaned in to flick his tongue over Zak's palm and taste the flavour of all three of them mixed together. It was sharp and sweet. It was nectar. He licked at it hungrily, occasionally tangling his tongue with Zak's as they worked together.

Finally, when Zak's hands where all clean, Lark stood back up and cuddled into Zak's side, closing his eyes even as he reached out and dragged Brody into the embrace.

As Brody leaned against the wall of Zak's broad chest, still panting for breath and fighting for control, he realised he had absolutely no idea where to go from here. What now? Were they lovers? Or were they just playing at hot, heavy and slightly kinky? Would he be able to live with that? Would he be able to live with only that, because as Brody looked between the two men, equally breathless and sated, he realised with disturbing clarity that their coming together had meant more than just getting their rocks off. At least it had for him. He had a true, deep and burning desire to get to know these beautiful, very different men. To spend time, not just in their bed, but getting to know and appreciate every aspect of them as individuals.

Brody had never felt that way before. Ever. He treated most people with suspicion and mistrust. He liked to keep them at a distance. But looking at Lark and Zak now, all well pleasured and smiling, he felt a tug in the region of his heart that demanded more from him than he had ever given before.

Oh, fuck! Now he really was in trouble. If he had been uneasy and confused before, his mind was damn near shutting down on him now, refusing to deal with any of it. He needed time. He needed space. He needed to get back to work.

"I...ahh...I better—"

Lark kissed Brody softly on the lips, smiling at him sweetly, and against all probability Brody felt his cock begin to stir weakly.

"It'll be okay, Brody. One day at a time."

Brody looked into Lark's huge, dark blue eyes and couldn't help but relax under his gentle, reassuring gaze.

"Sure," he murmured.

"Good man," Zak rumbled above him

He could do this. Whatever this was. He could do one day at a time. Sure. No problem. Sighing, he closed his eyes and rested his head back down on Zak's shoulder.

Brody knew he had to go or risk being caught by one of the others still working away in the kitchen, but he found he really didn't want to leave Zak's strength or Lark's warmth. He desperately hoped his heart got the memo about taking baby steps before it got all carried away. Unfortunately, he had the rather disturbing feeling it was already too late.

Chapter Seven

"They're sick!" Gus spat as he threw another dirty pan into the sink, slopping water over the edge and wetting the front of Brody's shirt in the process.

Brody closed his eyes for a second and clenched his jaw as he struggled not to react. He was still too new in the kitchen to make waves, and calling the mains chef an asshole right to his face probably wasn't ever going to be a good move for a lowly kitchen hand anyway.

"Just shut up, Gus," Dave shot back.

Ducking his head, Brody, began to scrub the bottom of the dirty pan industriously.

Tensions had been running high this evening. It had been a long, difficult shift, and Gus was more vocal than usual because he'd somehow messed up a stock order. They'd been forced to cancel one of their most popular dishes. Needless to say, Zak had not been happy, and Gus had been lashing out at everyone else in retaliation for the dressing down he'd received. Brody couldn't wait for the shift to finish.

"I'm just saying they're fucking sick," Gus continued irritably.

"Have you got a problem with them being gay?" Rio demanded, the tall, tanned man bristling and readying himself for a fight.

"Don't get your panties in a knot. I got no problem with 'alternative lifestyles'," Gus said, using his fingers to add little quote marks—which made him look utterly ridiculous, Brody thought as he continued to work on the pan.

"My problem is that they're brothers," Gus announced, and Brody froze mid-swipe of his scouring pad.

The entire kitchen froze. Absolute, unnerving silence fell over the area that was usually replete with a baffling array of sound.

"What the hell are you on about?" Rio finally snapped angrily.

"I said I don't give a shit that they're gay, but it's fucking sick that they're brothers."

Brody could hardly breathe. *No. It's not possible. It's just...is it? Could Zak and Lark be brothers? They didn't look—*

"You don't know what the fuck you're talking about," Rio said, turning away with a sneer of disgust.

"Hey! I've been here a hell of a lot longer than you have. I worked with their old man before he was killed in a pileup three years ago, and I know old man Piper always said his sons would inherit the place after he was gone."

"That doesn't mean that Zak and Lark are brothers," Dave interrupted, actually stopping what he was doing for once to join in on the conversation.

"You don't think? What about the fact they have the same last name. That didn't clue you all in?" Gus shot back, obviously thrilled to have an audience listening to him at last.

"They could be married," Rio suggested.

"They're not married, you dipstick. They're fucking brothers. Ha! Literally! Get it?"

Gus looked around, apparently pleased with his spontaneous wit and expecting everyone to appreciate it.

Brody clenched his jaw to stop himself from saying anything. What was going on? Was it true? And if it was, how did he feel about it? Hurt that they hadn't said anything? Angry? Disgusted?

Brody remembered the look that had passed between the two men when he had first met them. A look of utter love and contentment. And the passion he had witnessed as they made love in the office. No way could he think that was disgusting. In fact, it had been beautiful—and damn hot. Then there was the passion they had all shared in the storeroom this afternoon. He'd been thinking about little else all evening, wondering when he might have a chance to be with them both again. Had that suddenly changed for him? Would this news make a difference?

"Shut up, Gus. You don't know shit," Dave said.

"Gus wouldn't know shit from sugar. Why haven't you said anything before now if that's true, huh? " Andy added in a sarcastic drawl.

Gus's expression turned belligerent and mean. "Didn't want to say anything before now because I got bills to pay, and I don't mind taken their money. But I'm over it. I'd rather move back to Seattle and crash with my sister and her brats than put up with this shit!"

"Yeah, right, Gus. Whatever!" Andy replied. He turned away, too.

Brody tried to disappear into the background. He didn't want to be dragged into the whole, messy scene he could see unfolding before his eyes. He just needed a few seconds of peace to sort it all out. He wasn't sure what to believe. And what fucking business was it of anyone's anyway? Zak and Lark's personal life shouldn't be the subject of malicious kitchen gossip just because Gus was having a bad day. If only Gus would shut up, or at least leave him out of it.

Of course, his luck came up trumps again when Gus spied him standing quietly, scrubbing away at the already clean pan.

"What do you think, Brody? Don't you think it's fucking sick that Zak's screwing his baby brother?"

Brody shrugged absently, still struggling to work out what he felt. Two things sprang to mind immediately, however. One, he wasn't likely to get Gus to shut up by replying. Dickheads only fed off that sort of thing. And two, in his experience there were a whole lot more sick things in the world than two brothers loving each other.

Suddenly, Brody realised the kitchen had gone deathly silent again. With a sick sense of dread, he turned around and saw Zak's back as he stomped away. Lark stood in the doorway, his face a mask of barely restrained fury.

"Anytime you fuck-heads want to find yourselves another job, you go right ahead! In the meantime, you can all fuck off! Zak and I'll finish up. You all go home now and decide if you want to come back and keep your fucking mouths shut! Or you can pick up your paycheques at the end of the week."

Everyone stood and stared at the normally happy, laughing man that never had a cross or offensive word to say to anyone.

"I mean it. Get the fuck out. I don't want to see any of you till Tuesday. If then." With that Lark stalked away after Zak.

Brody felt as if his heart sank through his boots and seeped away across the floor into a puddle of shame.

"Oh, well done, shithead!" Dave shouted at Gus once Lark was gone. "Now we're all in trouble! Why can't you keep your big fucking mouth shut, asshole?"

"Why should I have to keep my mouth shut? And they didn't deny it, did they?" Gus tried to bluster, but his face was ashen and guilty.

"If I lose my job over this, you won't have to worry about keeping your mouth shut! It'll be wired closed because I'll break your stupid fucking jaw!" Dave screamed back.

"Okay! Everybody just cool it!" Rio yelled. "You heard the man! Everybody out!"

"They might be just a touchy-feely kind of family, dipshit," Andy broke in, angrily throwing a cloth he had been using to clean his hands down on the counter top.

"Oh, I've no doubt of that at all!" Gus said.

Rio pushed up his sleeves as if anticipating having to go toe-to-toe with Gus. "Shut up. Now, Gus."

"Just goes to show you what sort of a fucking mess the country's in when freaks like that can walk around owning businesses," Gus mumbled. He threw another dirty pan into the sink, splashing more water down Brody's front, and stormed off.

Brody just wished Gus would shut the fuck up and go home.

* * * *

Brody couldn't do it. He couldn't go home like this. He couldn't just leave knowing that Zak and Lark were angry with him. Worse still was the hurt he had seen in Lark's eyes. As if he had betrayed them somehow. And perhaps he had. He should have said something. He should have spoken up in their defence instead of standing there like a stunned mullet, trying not to get involved.

What was done was done, however, and Brody couldn't change that. But he knew he would drive himself absolutely insane with worry if he didn't go to them now. Brody couldn't leave things as they were for that long. He had to apologise. Explain. He needed to know what Zak and Lark were thinking. He had to talk to them now.

But, as Brody climbed the stairs on the outside of the building leading to the pair's apartment above the restaurant, he still wasn't exactly sure what he was going to say to them. What was there to say?

He was worried about losing his job. Sure. He could admit that. But that wasn't what was driving him on to what could turn out to be a very ugly scene with the two men. Brody couldn't let them think he thought they were disgusting. He didn't. Not in any way. Seeing the two of them together in the office had been one of the most beautiful, erotic things he had ever laid eyes on. And what they had shared with him earlier in the day...there were just no words to describe how incredible that experience had been. Just no words.

Growing up he had been exposed to some truly horrible things—at home, on the streets and in the various institutions that were supposed to be caring for him. Sex had often been a rushed, rough and mercenary affair, especially in the early days. But seeing Zak and Lark together, that had been something else entirely.

He'd begun to hope that maybe he'd be able to have a tiny taste of that difference himself. He was scared sure, but he wanted it.

Hesitantly, Brody knocked on the door and waited, holding his breath when he heard heavy footsteps on the other side. He knew it would be Zak. Lark's slight frame wouldn't be capable of such loud footfalls, no matter how angry or hurt he was. But it was still a shock when he was confronted with Zak's angry, stormy eyes looking down on him.

Looking up into Zak's hard, closed face, Brody realised no matter what he said he might not get a second chance. Perhaps he didn't deserve one. The sudden awareness made him feel physically ill.

"What?" Zak barked, completely blocking the doorway so he couldn't see whether Lark was there or not.

Brody swallowed. Hard. "Is Lark...I mean...I just—"

"Spit it out. If you're here to quit, fine. Just do it and get out."

"No! I mean, I need...I don't want to quit. I came to say I'm...I don't...I just..."

Brody wished he could see Lark. Talking to Zak like this was proving even more difficult than he had first thought. He really didn't want to have to do it all over again with Lark.

"What, Brody? You don't want to be with us anymore? Is that it? You want to forget we ever touched you?" Zak's voice was clipped and tight, and he gripped the doorframe until his knuckles were white.

"No!" Brody cried out in alarm, afraid that Zak was about to slam the door in his face. "I don't. I mean I do. I do want you." Brody took a deep breath and struggled to order his thoughts before Zak kick him down the stairs for his inept fumbling for the right words. "I do want to be with you. I think you and Lark are amazing together. I really...yeah."

Brody felt completely lame as he tried to express how he felt. It was all tied up in knots, and for a moment, Zak just stared at him, as if he wasn't going to give Brody an inch. Then Zak seemed to deflate right before his eye, all the fight and anger draining away until all that was left was a tired, worn, and...fragile looking man.

Brody wouldn't have believed Zak could ever look fragile. He was so big and muscular and...well, solid. His demeanour was one of strength and confidence and leadership. But at the moment, Zak looked like the slightest thing would tip him over the edge. Brody wanted to reach out, wrap his arms around the man and hold him close. But he wasn't quite sure he'd earned that right yet.

"It just...it blindsided me. It was just so..." Even as he tried to explain, Brody began to realise two things.

First, it really didn't matter. He didn't care at all if Zak and Lark were brothers. The only thing that really mattered to him was that they were two of the hottest, sweetest, most genuinely caring men he'd ever met, and they were interested in him. And he was incredibly interested right back.

The second thing Brody knew was that he had to somehow make it right between them all again. That would be his first priority. He pushed everything else away to focus on that one goal.

"Zak?" Lark asked from somewhere behind the big man blocking the doorway. Zak searched Brody's face for a moment, as if wanting to make absolutely certain he wasn't going to hurt Lark somehow, before he stepped back.

Brody's heart ached when he saw Lark, whose eyes were red-rimmed and swollen from crying. Lark had always smiled. To see the broken, dejected look on his face was even harder than confronting Zak's anger.

"It's alright, Lark. Brody is…" Zak's voice trailed off as if he wasn't quite sure what to say about what Brody was doing there at the moment.

Brody had to admit he wasn't sure what to say either. He just knew he couldn't leave things the way they were. Without giving himself time to stop and think about what he was doing, Brody took a step forward and wrapped his arms around Lark.

"I'm sorry, Lark. I'm so sorry! I should have said something. I should have defended you, told Gus to shut his stupid mouth. Something!"

"I thought…when you didn't…" Lark's voice was muffled against his chest, but Brody could hear the stress in it. And he couldn't stand it, not from Lark. Lark should never be like this.

Pulling away, Brody tilted Lark's face up to capture his lips in a deep, aggressive kiss, trying to erase the torment and anguish he sensed in the other man. He wanted to take all the hurt and pain of the evening away and replace it with warmth and passion. Within seconds, Lark was thrusting his tongue back to meet Brody. Licking and moaning and nipping at him just as fiercely.

Brody felt the explosive power of the kiss ignite other fires within his body. Soon he was a raging inferno of lust and desire and something else, something that was slowly sneaking in while they were busy feeding the flames of their need for one another. But for the moment Brody tried to ignore the niggling sensation. For the moment his body was in complete control and demanding more.

Just as he was about to start working on the buttons of Lark's shirt he felt Zak wrap his arms around the two of them and drag them inside. The heavy slam of the door echoed in the room.

Zak pushed them both, still clinging and grinding against one another, back against the wall. There was nothing gentle or tender or soft about Zak now. He was all aggressive, sharp movements and feral intensity. And it drove Brody absolutely wild to see Zak lose control like this. To feel Zak tearing at him, pulling at his shirt, yanking at his fly buttons — it was incredible.

"I want to see. I want Lark to fuck you while I fuck him. Show me you want us together like that." Zak punctuated his demands with a stinging little nip to Brody's bottom lip that had him arching up into Zak and crying out with his arousal.

"Yes," Brody hissed before Zak sealed their lips together again.

As Brody let Zak thrust his tongue in to explore his mouth and answered eagerly with his own voracious exploration, Lark was rubbing and stroking his hands over them. Lark nuzzled into them, leaving open mouthed kisses and sucking gently on their necks and any expanse of skin left exposed where their shirts had been opened by questing hands and ripped buttons.

Lark pulled away from them unexpectedly, but before he could take more than two steps, Zak yanked him back.

"Where do you think you're going?"

"Condoms. Lube. We need—" Lark's eyes blazed as he raised himself up onto his toes to plant loud, smacking kisses between the words on Zak's lips.

Zak growled, pulled Lark in tighter to his body and drove the last kiss into a true, passionate claiming. As if Zak couldn't stand the thought of Lark leaving them even for the short time it would take to get supplies.

Completely mindless with lust now and not wanting to be left out, Brody licked at their joined mouths until they made room for him to merge with them.

Still holding on to both of them, Zak began to walk them all through to the next room, pausing as they went at a hall table. Without breaking away from them, Zak tugged open a drawer and scrabbled about in it. He pulled out a bottle of lube then continued to dig around. Finally, Zak pulled away and slapped the drawer closed in frustration.

"Naked. Now," he commanded. He glared at Brody and Lark with a fierce, hungry look. Whatever he saw satisfied him, and he turned to stalk away.

Brody shivered and quickly shed his clothes; Lark did the same beside him. When Brody was fully naked, he looked up again to see that Zak had returned with a ribbon of condoms dangling from his fingers. Soon, Zak was shucking off his own shirt and jeans. As each new delicious inch of Zak's body was revealed, Brody felt his cock throb. The broad, hairy chest, the firm, bulging muscles of his legs, arms, and abs, the long, thick cock that pulsed, leaking beads of clear pre-cum and glistening invitingly—Zak was magnificent in every way.

Zak shoved gently but insistently on his shoulder. "On the couch, Brody, let us take care of you."

Brody glanced around to the matte black leather couch behind them. Yes. This was what he wanted, here with these two stunning men. Now.

He focussed on Lark. He was so completely different in form and feature to Zak. Lark was all slim, lean muscle and pale, smooth skin. The tousled mop of his blond hair fell into his eyes and begged to be brushed back. Brody reached out, grasped Lark's wrist and pulled him over to the couch.

Brody lay down and stretched out on the butter-soft leather, then guided Lark to lie over him. He took another long, drugging kiss and thrust up into the warm welcoming body as Lark settled onto him. Their cocks met and moved over one another, their pre-cum smearing and coating both of them with a thin, slippery film.

Cool, wet fingers touched Brody's hole, making him gasp and jerk as Zak spread lube in lazy circles around his hole. Brody opened his legs wider and pushed back, trying to get more, dying to feel Zak's thick fingers enter him.

"Shh, baby. I've got you. I've got you both. My beautiful boys," Zak whispered.

Lark shuddered and Brody imagined Zak was doing the same thing to both of them, swirling his fingers around in a teasing, gentle touch to soothe and relax their muscles so they could all play together. But the sensation was always just too damn frustratingly light to truly satisfy.

Slowly, a thick finger breached him and Brody joined Lark in a lust-filled moan of pleasure. The finger moved in and out of him—fast, then slow, straight, then in ever-widening rotations. Then, with a second finger, Zak began to scissor him open, slowly stretching and preparing him. Lark wriggled and moaned above him in shared bliss.

As best he could, Brody kept his eyes open and locked on Lark's face. They communicated wordlessly the wonder and joy that Zak gave to them. Finally, a third thick finger pushed in. Brody threw back his head and arched up into Lark in ecstasy. He was so perfectly stretched and filled.

"Zak! Oh! Ah! Lark...want..."

Brody couldn't find the words. Zak continued to thrust his fingers in and out, rotating and spreading him—creating lightning that flashed through his body whenever the clever fingers brushed over the sweet, sensitive spot deep inside him.

Lark was no better off. His cock leaked copious strings of pre-cum onto Brody's belly, which were quickly smeared and rubbed away as Lark thrust and writhed against him.

"Zak, please, I need you," Lark eventually begged, eyes closed as he panted for breath.

"Okay, baby," Zak cooed.

Brody heard the tearing of condom packets, but was surprised when he felt Zak envelop his cock in the thin latex as well. Looking up, Brody saw Lark watching him with the hottest smile he'd ever seen. It somehow managed to be both cheeky and filled with passion at the same time.

"Leather," Lark whispered. "Zak's very protective of his couch. That's why we have condoms in the living room."

Brody heard the sharp slap of Zak's palm on the unprotected flesh of Lark's backside. Lark yelped, but the smile on his face broadened into a huge grin. Brody chuckled.

"We'll see if you're still laughing when Lark's pounding your ass while I pound his," Zak warned, but it was all show. Brody could hear the joy in the man's voice.

"Mmmm, yeah! Want it, Zak," Lark said. He wriggled back and sat up a little so he could roll a condom onto his long, slender shaft. Then he climbed back over Brody and positioned himself at Brody's hole.

"Ready, baby?" Lark asked huskily.

"Please," Brody begged.

The tip of Lark's cock touched his hole and Brody bucked up into it. The feeling of that first contact and the delicious pressure of Lark's cock head against him was pure ecstasy. He needed more.

"Oh! Oh, move! Please, Lark, fuck me!"

Lark steadily pushed in, using his hand to guide his cock in a long slow thrust. Brody closed his eyes and threw back his head even though he desperately wanted to watch Lark sink into him for the very first time. When Lark was all the way inside, he stopped to let Brody adjust and allow them both time to savour the sensation. All too soon it wasn't enough.

"More!"

Lark began to thrust into Brody, tentatively at first, then gradually increasing to long, slow strokes. The exquisite drag of Lark's cock in and out of Brody's hole was so agonizingly sweet that Brody found himself grinding his pelvis back into Lark's groin, trying to help Lark reach deeper inside him.

Brody was nearly mindless with lust and need now, but also very aware that more than half of what he was feeling was because it was Lark doing this to him. Not some stranger in a dark alley, but Lark—the amazing, bright, bubbly, happy man who sent his heart racing whenever he stepped into a room, or flashed one of his trademark killer smiles at him.

Lark moaned, thrust himself balls deep into Brody's hole and stilled. Brody looked up and saw Zak's larger body covering Lark from behind. With infinite care, Zak curled over them to lay tender kisses and licks to Lark's long, arched neck.

Zak looked more beautiful than ever this way—a tender giant offering himself to Lark. Brody's heart beat a frantic tattoo as he watched the two of them together. How could anyone think this was disgusting? Never!

Then Zak began to move. *He's fucking Lark while Lark's in me!* It was almost too much to take in and believe.

Zak fucked in long, smooth strokes, just the way Lark had begun. Zak's broad, tanned hands came to rest against Lark's pale hips to guide Lark in and out of Brody. They all began to move with the same even, synchronised rhythm. Endlessly they moved and loved together.

Gradually, their movements became less co-ordinated and more primal, more feral and intense. Thrusts became shoves. Moans became grunts. Faster and faster they drove into one another until at last Brody felt himself teetering on the edge of an orgasmic precipice.

"Oh! Oh! Lark, Zak. Gonna...Ahhhh!" Brody exploded into the thin, latex barrier, his cock throbbing and filling it with spurt after spurt of thick, white cream.

Lark thrust into Brody one last time and cried out in ecstasy. Brody felt the cock in his ass pulse as the orgasm rocketed through his lover's body, spilling heavy shots of seed into the condom. The sensation of

Lark's cock shooting inside him set off another, weaker round of ejaculation from Brody's cock. Then Zak bellowed out his own release and Brody watched in awe as he came inside Lark.

Sated and exhausted, Lark and Zak carefully withdrew. Then Lark collapsed down on top of Brody and Zak lay down on his side at the very edge of the couch.

Zak didn't look terribly comfortable for the long term, but Brody wiggled across weakly with Lark still on top of him and made as much room as possible. He didn't want to lose the close, connected feeling he had with his lovers just yet.

"You know," Lark murmured against Brody's chest, "if we keep this up, Brody's going to think we don't own a bed."

Zak chuckled — a sleepy, husky sound that, if he was a cat, Brody was sure would have made him purr.

They all lay tangled together, their bodies slowly cooling and their breathing gradually returning to normal. Zak gently stroked is hand down Lark's back. The smaller man nuzzled into Brody and groaned softly at the tender attention.

"We do, you know," Lark eventually continued. "Do you want to see it? You could stay the night."

Brody tensed. He'd stayed too long as it was. He needed to get back home to Wolf. "I'm sorry. I have to…I have to go."

Struggling to sit up, he deeply regretted disturbing the delicious post-coital snuggle they had going on, and Lark's pitiful whine at his insistence that they let him up only added to Brody's torment. He really didn't want to go anywhere. His well-loved and sated body was heavy and slow. It tempted Brody to collapse back into their arms, where he knew he would be welcome to stay until morning. And probably more than welcome to join them in another round or two of fucking before then. But he fought it off.

"Stay," Zak insisted, reaching out with a light, restraining hand to capture Brody's wrist.

"Please stay. Just for a little while," Lark added, leaning forward to place a soft, tender kiss along the line of Brody's lower jaw, taking the time to add a tiny lick against the faint hint of his stubble.

Brody shuddered a little and closed his eyes, but he managed to shake his head in denial. He really couldn't. "I'm sorry. I really…I have to go. I want to stay, believe me. It's just…I have to go. I'll…can I come back tomorrow night? At least for a little while? I just…I need to go now."

The seconds of silence that followed unnerved Brody to the point of caving in and begging them to let him stay. What would he do if they ended it right here and now because he couldn't give them this? Couldn't give them all night?

The way Zak and Lark were looking at him right now, a little concerned and perhaps a touch hurt, as if they were struggling not to take his refusal personally, almost weakened Brody's resolve. But finally, Zak broke the tension and saved him from being completely irresponsible.

"Of course you can," Zak reassured, gently pulling Lark away and back into his arms so Brody could finally get up and start dressing. "You're welcome here anytime. For as long as you can give us. We'll always want you here."

Brody shivered at those words. Zak couldn't have said anything more precious — or made it any more difficult for Brody to leave. Curse the gorgeous bastard! But Brody steeled himself against the longing looks and tempting warmth of the men curling up into the corner of the couch. He began to search for his scattered clothing. He had to go. At least for now.

* * * *

Lark was sad to watch Brody trudge down the stairs from their apartment before heading off into the night. He wished they could have at least dropped him home. But Brody would have said no, so in the end Lark hadn't even asked.

Lark closed the door quietly and leaned against the frame for a moment. It had been one hell of a crazy night. He didn't ever want to walk in on a scene like the one in the kitchen tonight. Not ever again.

Man, the look on Zak's face had nearly killed him. But it had also been an astonishing turning point in their relationship with Brody. So although hearing their new lover say he had to go certainly wasn't what Lark had wanted to hear, at least now they had moved on from uncertainty and frustration.

Lark wished Brody had reconsidered and stayed with them though. He wanted the man here – in their arms, in their bed. Lark wanted them all to ride the wild, exciting lust while it was still new and fresh until they couldn't move. But at the same time, Lark had heard how much Brody really did regret having to leave, and that gave him some small measure of peace and a sense of victory. The need obviously wasn't one-sided. And Brody had asked to come back. That had to be a good sign.

And instead of running from them when he'd heard what Gus had said about them, Brody had come to them. He'd opened his heart and accepted them, warts and all, regardless of whether the rumour was true or not. That meant everything to Lark.

Yes, he'd been hurt when Brody had shrugged instead of telling Gus to go fuck himself. But Lark suspected that it was just Brody's way. He didn't seem to like confrontation. And if Brody could accept the suggestion of something as taboo as incest, then Lark figured he could accept a casual shrug.

Then of course there was what had happened after Brody came to them this evening. That had been incredible. No doubt about it. And there had been a lot more than just animal lust and attraction going on.

Unfortunately, Lark was also more certain than ever that Brody was hiding something. Of course, Lark wanted to know everything right here and now. And more than that, he wanted to jump right in and fix whatever was wrong. But Brody's secrets were his to tell, not Lark's to pry out of him with a crowbar. And just as Lark and Zak were big enough to fight their own battles with idiots like Gus, Brody was a man and they couldn't interfere where they were not yet welcome.

It just made Lark all the more determined to get to know Brody, and for Brody to get to know them. Perhaps then he would allow them to help. Before it was too late. Before one, or all of them was hurt by whatever Brody wasn't telling them.

Chapter Eight

Brody wasn't exactly sure what he was doing at the restaurant today—on Monday, everyone's day off. He'd made arrangements to come back to see Lark and Zak tonight, but when Wolf had gone for a nap Brody simply hadn't been able to resist coming to see them again. It had pulled at him until he finally gave in and walked the few blocks to the restaurant.

He knew he wouldn't be able to stay long, maybe an hour at the most, but he wanted those sixty minutes with his lovers.

His lovers. Brody tried out the sound of it, repeating it over and over in his brain. Tasting and assessing it. Finding he really liked the idea.

Seeing the back door to the restaurant flung open, probably to let much-needed cool air into the stuffy kitchen, Brody veered away from the stairs to the apartment and opted for trying his luck in the restaurant itself. It was a pretty good bet that if one was there, he'd find them both. Zak and Lark seemed to be rarely apart. Brody was glad he wouldn't have to waste precious minutes of his free time searching them out.

Quietly stepping into the kitchen, he peeked into the office and spotted Zak hunched over and hard at work at the small, scarred office desk. Surrounded by an ocean of paperwork, Zak looked busy and frustrated, as he ran his hands over the short bristles of his hair and huffed out a tired breath. Lark was nowhere to be seen.

Brody began to worry that maybe he should leave. Zak looked like he'd rather not be disturbed right now. And Brody wasn't sure about the idea of just the two of them being together without Lark around. Maybe that was some sort of boundary he didn't know about yet.

But just as he was about to turn and hurry away, Zak looked up and Brody's chance to slip away was lost.

"Brody!"

"Um...hi."

"What are you doing here?"

"I'm sorry. I can see you're busy. I'll just go."

"No!" Zak stood up and hurried over. He enfolded Brody in a tight hug, clasping him against a hard wall of muscle.

For a second, Brody closed his eyes and breathed Zak's warm, spicy scent in. It was a smell that was becoming more familiar every day and had started to make him half-hard now whenever he caught a hint of it. It was all male musk with a touch of something spicy. And Brody was falling in love with it.

"Hi," Zak breathed.

"Hi," Brody replied, struggling to keep his voice even and casual when all he wanted to do was rip the man's clothes off.

"I'm glad you dropped by."

"You are?"

"Yeah."

Zak leaned in and placed a chaste kiss on Brody's lips. It ended all too quickly. So Brody pulled Zak down and took another one. A second light kiss led to a third, and by the fourth, neither of them could hold back from opening their mouths to deepen it to something more thorough. More satisfying.

Exploring and tasting every inch of Zak's mouth, Brody pressed into Zak's solid warmth until there wasn't enough room to squeeze a slip of Zak's long forgotten paperwork between them. They rubbed and clung and moaned together until the need for air forced them to part.

Zak sank to his knees, and Brody's heart pounded hard and fast in his chest.

"Zak? What—"

"Want to taste you," Zak murmured as he worked open the buttons of Brody's pants.

Brody's cock sprang free to bounce against his belly. It seemed Zak's kiss had already made Brody's cock start to drool as much as his mouth. A drop of pre-cum smeared into his shirt, but Brody didn't care. All his concentration was focussed on the sight of Zak carefully adjusting Brody's pants and boxers until his cock and balls were perfectly exposed above the waistbands.

"Zak I don't—"

"Shh, just enjoy."

Zak used the tip of his tongue to lick up the pre-cum from the slit of Brody's cock. Brody threw back his head and thrust his hips forward helplessly.

It wasn't that no one had ever gone down on him before. It just wasn't something that had happened often. Brody was accustomed to being the one expected to give this pleasure, not the one who received it. He wasn't exactly sure what to do. His hands wanted to run over the stiff bristles of Zak's crew cut. He wanted to thrust into Zak's mouth, to fuck into it until he came. But he wasn't sure how Zak would feel about that.

Then the sensation of Zak's hot, wet mouth closing over his shaft and swallowing him down to the root overwhelmed Brody.

"Zak! Ah! Stop, Zak, I can't—"

Zak's mouth released him and Brody was so conflicted about whether that was a good thing or not, he missed the first few words his lover whispered to him.

"—got you." Zak licked at Brody's shaft again as if he couldn't wait to get back to it. "Just relax. Let me."

Zak's mouth sank back down over his cock, and Brody watched this time as more and more of his hard shaft disappeared between the man's lips. Zak's cheeks hollowed a little as he sucked him in. Then Brody saw him swallow and felt the smooth walls of Zak's throat caress the head of his cock.

"Ah! Fuck! Zak!" Brody couldn't help himself, he had to reach out and cradle Zak's head between his hands as the man continued to suck and lave and deep throat his desperate cock.

Brody didn't try to move or manipulate Zak in any way. He just used the feel of the fine, spiked hair brushing against his palms and fingers to ground himself as he began to wind up for one almighty orgasmic release.

"Ah, fuck! Ah, fuck!" Brody chanted, before finally bellowing Zak's name.

Brody couldn't restrain it any more. He thrust into Zak's hot, welcoming mouth and came in long, continuous gushes of seed that Zak swallowed eagerly. Jerk after jerk of his shaft emptied his balls until Brody was spent.

When Brody found that he was holding Zak's head pressed to his groin. He gasped and released Zak, afraid he might have gone too far, been too physical. Zak simply smiled up at Brody and licked his lips before surging to his feet.

Brody's heart swelled with emotion. He pulled Zak into a bone-crushing hug. His breath came in panting gasps and his legs trembled. Sex had never been anything more than physical. What the two of them had just shared was far more. Brody could only lean into his lover and wait for his heart to slow and his mind to catch up.

"I…I, ah…" Brody tried after a few seconds.

"Yeah, me too." Zak's voice was steady, but husky and Brody heard him clear his throat.

Brody wriggled as he tried to get down on his knees so he could start relieving Zak. *The man's probably cursing up a storm in his head right now because I haven't started on his blow job already.* But Zak only tightened his arm when Brody tried to kneel down.

"What's wrong?" Zak asked with a concerned look on his face.

"I…um…I just thought you…you know?"

For a moment, Zak looked at him, carefully scrutinising him until Brody felt an almost overwhelming need to squirm. It became difficult to maintain eye contact.

"I'm fine," Zak finally said, pulling him close again and taking a deep breath. But Brody could feel the steel-hard ridge of Zak's erection pressed against him.

"Don't you want me to...?"

"Not right now. I just want to hold you for a second."

"But—"

"Shh." Zak said, squeezing him a little. "That was just for you. You don't have to do me because I did you."

Brody didn't understand, but he couldn't really argue. Especially when being held by Zak and losing himself in the solid warmth and tempting strength of Zak's arms was so compelling. It just felt so right, so...perfect.

"But—"

"Shh." Zak kissed the top of his head lightly and squeezed again.

"Will you let me make it up to you tonight?" Brody eventually asked, not just wanting to reciprocate now, but truly wanting Zak. He wanted to take the thick cock he could feel pressed up against him into his mouth and demonstrate his desire. It was a very new, very heady sensation that made Brody almost drunk with the delightful feeling it created inside him.

"Mmmm, I'd like that." It was almost as if Zak sensed the difference, had wanted him to come to this point all along—not just returning the favour, but wanting it.

Brody felt blessed and so lucky to have found Zak and Lark. To be allowed a chance, a window of time — however small—to be with them and to get to know them. He couldn't believe he had resisted for so long before taking the leap. Worse still, he'd almost lost the chance completely because of someone else's stupid, malicious gossip, when it was really none of their business.

"I could never think of you or Lark as disgusting, or what you have together as wrong. I think...I think it's...beautiful."

The words tumbled out of him without any conscious decision on Brody's part. The easy, relaxed mood began to evaporate around them and Brody really didn't understand why. He only knew that he could have kicked himself for bring it all up and making Zak look distinctly uncomfortable so soon after his mind-blowing orgasm.

Wanting to reclaim some of the ease there had been between them before he'd opened his big mouth, Brody tried to change the subject. "So why are you working today anyway? I thought Lark had a strict 'no working on days off' rule." Brody had thought Zak would come back with a retort about how bossy Lark was, or how it was good for the man not to get his own way all the time. Instead, Zak sobered and pulled away even more. "What's wrong?" Brody asked — really worried by the serious, dark look he saw in Zak's eyes now.

"Gus quit. That's why I'm in here. I have to find a replacement fast. We've got a huge weekend booked and even with me filling in, we're still going to need an extra set of hands."

Huh! Brody couldn't say he was sorry to see Gus go, but... What a prick! He caused trouble while he was here, then quit and caused trouble when he was gone. But Brody was more concerned by the way Zak was looking at the moment. The stiff, brooding way he concentrated on straightening his clothes. There was a world of things Zak wasn't saying about Gus's decision to quit and the whole situation. He suspected it was the real crux of his sudden silence. Brody just wanted to make things all better somehow, but he wasn't sure how he could do that. Or even how to broach the subject.

"I know I haven't done much prep, but I'd be happy to come in early and help, if I can." It wasn't much, and it wasn't even scratching at whatever the deeper issue was that had Zak looking so hurt and solemn. But Zak smiled at him anyway, and something inside Brody eased at the sight of it.

"Thanks, babe. That would help. We're still going to be short, but…that helps a lot."

The way Zak looked at him made Brody think he meant more than just the offer to help out in the kitchen. Brody felt his cheeks heat in a blush at the soft, adoring way Zak was looking at him. It was almost the same look he saw on Zak's face sometimes when he looked at Lark.

With a jolt, Brody realised he wanted that. It might not happen now or even next week. It might never happen. But Brody wanted more than anything for Zak to look at him like that…forever.

Zak looked away. "You know, about what Gus said—"

Brody was just about to interrupt him—to tell him it didn't matter, that he really didn't care—when they heard a loud bang against the wall as something heavy smashed into the building.

"What the hell?" Zak shouted.

Together they rushed outside, just in time to hear the squeal of tyres from around the side of the building. Zak took off running and Brody tried to follow, but the bigger man was too fast. A few seconds later Zak jogged back to him, his brows furrowed in irritation.

"Did you see who it was?" Brody asked as Zak continued towards him.

"Nah! They were too quick. Probably just kids—" Zak froze. He was looking back towards the restaurant's loading area. A stunned look of disbelief crossed his face then faded to anger. "What the fuck!"

Brody spun around to see what had caught Zak's attention. Bright red paint dripped down the wall like blood from a bad horror movie. But the real horror was the phrase 'YOU SICK FREAKS!' scrawled in large letters across the building. The bang had obviously been the tin hitting the wall as a final angry act to punctuate the obscene vandalism.

"Oh, Zak!"

"Help me get it off. I don't want Lark to see it."

"But shouldn't we call the police?"

"No."

"But—"

"Brody, I don't want every nut job and media hound in the district camped out on my doorstep, making our lives miserable. And that's what would happen if this got out." Zak angrily gestured to the wet paint mess.

"It had to be someone from last night. Someone from the kitchen."

"Maybe. I don't know. Maybe someone said something to someone else and they did this. I just don't know. We just have to wait and see what happens. If we start getting more and more people making trouble, I'll deal with it then. Right now I just want to get this mess cleaned up so Lark doesn't see it. He was upset enough last night without this shit."

"Do you think it was Gus?"

"Who knows? Who fuckin' cares?" Zak ran a shaking hand over his head as if he was about to lose it.

Brody draped his arm over Zak's huge shoulders. The angle was slightly weird because Zak was so much taller, but it still felt good, so he didn't pull away. "Don't worry. We'll get it cleaned up. Lark won't have to know anything."

"Thanks," Zak said wearily as he leaned into Brody a little. Zak's acceptance of his embrace and support made Brody feel about a mile high.

"I want to protect him too, Zak. I don't ever want Lark getting hurt. Especially not like this. He's too..."

"Yeah, I know. He is. I've always known he was."

* * * *

Tuesday came bright and clear. And far too quickly, as far as Lark was concerned. On Mondays—their one day off a week—he always tried to make a complete break from the restaurant. And he insisted Zak do the same. But it had been a complete and utter disaster this week. Not only had Zak spent the entire day trying to replace Gus, but it also turned out Gus hadn't just forgotten to order some ingredients. He'd actually pissed the suppliers off so much that they had refused to deal with Sandpipers anymore.

What a fiasco. Lark had spent the day trying to soothe and placate the aggrieved suppliers. At least the restaurant was back in their good books now. But what a waste of his time when it could all so easily have been avoided if Gus hadn't been such an asshole.

Worst of all, though, had been when Brody called to take a rain cheque on coming over. He'd said something had come up at home and he had to stay in.

Lark had wanted to help. He wanted to go around to Brody's house right away to see what they could do.

And, okay, he wanted to know what was going on with the other man. But Zak had been his usual, firm, patient self and made him stay put and wait for Brody to open up to them in his own sweet time. Damn obstinate, principled man.

And now this. Lark looked back down at the single sheet of paper. So innocuous looking in its crisp, white, unmarked envelope. Lark felt like screwing it up and hurling it across the room as far away from himself as possible.

"Hey, Lark! What's happening?"

Lark jumped a little when Brody stepped into the office to join him, but quickly recovered.

"Nothing." Folding the paper, Lark carefully placed it back into its envelope before tucking it away into his back pocket.

"Is everything all right?" Brody asked, his brow creasing into a worried frown.

Shit. Time for a distraction. Brody didn't need to know or worry about what was in the letter.

"Sure. Have you seen Zak?" Lark asked casually.

Brody started to look distinctly uncomfortable. "No. Why?"

Bingo.

Lark shrugged. "Zak mentioned you stopped in the other day when I wasn't here. I just wondered if you'd caught up with him today, too."

"Oh! Fuck!" was all Brody could manage to say.

Lark chuckled and smiled wickedly. "Yeah, well, he told me about that too." When the blood drained from Brody's face, Lark felt like an asshole. He hadn't meant to upset, just distract. He stepped forward and pulled Brody into a hug. "Hey, it's okay. It's fine. Really. I'm not mad or anything. Are you okay?"

Brody could only nod, and Lark ran his hands up and down his strong, lean back, and settled his head against Brody's chest. It was a comforting hug, meant for Brody's sake, but Lark found himself taking an equal measure of solace in it. It was just what he needed right now. Lark nuzzled into the soft material of Brody's shirt and squeezed a little.

"Sorry. I didn't mean for you to think I was upset about it. I'm fine with you and Zak having time together, just the two of you," Lark said.

"You sure? I'm sorry about cancelling last night. I..." The worried sound creeping in around the edges of Brody's voice had Lark tightening his arms around the other man and wanting to kick his own ass for putting it there.

"I'm sure," Lark reiterated firmly, "And it's fine about last night. Did everything work out at home?"

"Yeah, everything's fine again."

Lark gave Brody plenty of time to add more, but after a while it was obvious the man wasn't going to offer anything voluntarily. Lark tried to rein in his frustration and changed the subject, deciding to take a leaf from Zak's book and not push.

"Actually, I wanted to say thanks. Zak told me what you said, about...about the two of us being together. It means a lot to us that you're not disgusted. That you don't leap to judging us."

"I could never think badly of either of you."

"Who says I'm not bad!" Lark fired back in mock outrage, trying to lighten the mood.

"I think you're gorgeous." The bright blush that flared into Brody's cheeks as he said it was absolutely adorable and Lark leaned up and kissed one hot, red cheek simply because he couldn't help himself.

Snuggling back in to enjoy a few more moments cuddling before they had to get to work, Lark brought his head down to rest against Brody's chest and listened to the steady drum of the heart beneath his ear.

"You really don't mind?" Brody asked unexpectedly.

"What?"

"That Zak and I…you know."

Lark leant back and looked up into Brody's still tight, worried expression. That just wouldn't do. He took Brody's lips in a searing, passionate kiss and lost himself in sharing his breath with Brody — in stroking over his tongue and exploring the warm, wet cavern of his mouth. He forgot about vegetable prep, about the letter, about whatever secrets Brody was keeping. Everything. The only thing that existed was Brody, held in the tight circle of his arms, and their open, hungry mouths.

Brody relaxed into the kiss and moaned mournfully when Lark pulled away for them to catch a breath. As they stared into each other's lust-clouded eyes, Lark ran his hand over Brody's face, pushing back the slightly overlong bangs of his fringe.

"Does that answer your question?" Lark whispered against Brody's lips.

"Yeah. Pretty much." Brody leant down and licked at the seam of Lark's lips again.

As their mouths joined together in another long, drugging kiss, Brody reached down and rubbed his hand across the front of Lark's pants, massaging the hard length of his cock through the layers of material.

Lark groaned and thrust forward helplessly. Jerking his head away, he sucked in a deep lungful of air to try to calm himself down.

"Oh, man! We have to stop, or I'm going to come in my pants!" Lark gasped, but he couldn't bring himself to actually make Brody stop.

"You live right upstairs. You could always go change." Brody sounded just as eager to continue.

"But the others will be here any moment to start prep."

"I don't want to stop," Brody pleaded, still rubbing a little, but slowing the movement down in deference to Lark's point.

Looking up, Lark saw Brody's eyes heavy with lust and his thin, dark pink lips parted invitingly. Brody obviously wasn't thinking straight and it was almost more temptation than Lark could resist. Almost. But he didn't want Brody to get mixed up in the ugly possibilities of the kitchen right now. And if they were caught like this, he would be.

Stepping back, Lark put some much-needed distance between them. The longing, passionate look gradually faded from Brody's face to be replaced with confusion. But Lark hardened his heart just a little.

The ugliness Gus had started the other night wasn't over yet. No one knew it better than Lark. And Brody...well Brody just didn't understand. Not completely. It wouldn't be fair to expose him to it all before he knew what he was getting into.

To be honest, Lark wasn't entirely sure about Brody either. He did know he didn't want the younger man getting hurt if it started getting out of hand — which it had every possibility of doing. But Brody was still largely a mystery to them. He didn't really know much about the man at all.

Lark stared at Brody for a minute.

"You never even asked if it was true," Lark pointed out, wondering why Brody hadn't broached the subject of Gus's allegations.

But Brody simply shrugged and looked completely uninterested.

"Doesn't it bother you?"

After seeming to consider the idea carefully for a moment, Brody shook his head. "No. Not really. I mean there are a lot of terrible things happening in the world. The way you and Zak are together isn't one on them. That's beautiful. I just wish..." Brody looked away, and no matter how hard Lark willed him to continue, he didn't.

"You know, Zak and I —"

Brody sealed Lark's lips by gently placing a finger over them. "You don't need to explain anything, Lark. It doesn't matter. Really. I don't care."

Slowly, Lark began to nod. He didn't really want to get into it at the moment, either. Brody's easy acceptance of them either way was a balm to his soul, especially now, with everything so tense with their co-workers in the kitchen.

"You going to be able to come over tonight?" Lark asked instead.

"Um...yeah...sure...for a bit anyway."

"Good." Lark straightened his clothes, repositioning his cock as it began to settle back down, albeit reluctantly. "You know, this week's day off was such a complete write-off I'm thinking of doing something special next Monday. Getting right away from the place and having some fun. Do you want to come with us?"

Lark saw the hesitation, a tension that stiffened Brody's shoulders.

"I...can I think about it? I'm just not sure I can make it this coming Monday."

There was definitely something holding Brody back. Something significant, if Lark was any judge, and it was slowly driving him up the wall to see it and know that Brody wasn't telling them something important.

Lark let it go for now, but there was going to be a time in the not so distant future, when no matter what Zak said, or how much Brody tried to avoid telling them, that Lark wouldn't let him get away with being evasive. For now he let the matter go.

"Sure." Lark shrugged like it wasn't a big deal, but it was becoming one. One that needed to be put to rest. There were just a few more important things that needed to be sorted out first. But after that, he was going to do some serious digging, and he wouldn't rest until he had some answers.

Chapter Nine

Zak was trying to read a novel. AR Piper – one of his favourite authors. He loved losing himself in the convoluted plots and unexpected twists that had become her trademark. But Lark wasn't making it easy.

As if prompted by the thought, Lark stretched out his legs along the length of the couch and pushed his feet under Zak's ass, burrowing his cold toes beneath and snuggling back into the cushions with a contented sigh.

"Ever get the feeling you're being used?" Zak grumbled as he flicked another page over without looking up.

"Shut up. That's the most useful thing your ass has done all day!" Lark quipped as he closed his eyes with a cheeky grin and snuggled down further into the cushions.

Zak growled, but didn't stir himself any more than that. He was far too tired and comfortable and it wouldn't do any good anyway – he was bound to lose whatever argument might start up between them. Besides, he didn't exactly mind having Lark's feet where they were, so what was the point.

Having lost his place, Zak found his concentration drifting to thoughts of the day. Overall, it had been a remarkably good one—unlike last Monday. Today Lark had insisted they take a proper day off, right away from the restaurant. They'd spent it on the beach, lazing in the sun and occasionally cooling off in the rolling waves of the ocean. It had been a magnificent way to unwind and de-stress. Zak hadn't felt so relaxed and calm in ages. The only thing missing had been Brody.

Having spent all week slaving away with him in the kitchen, then at least an hour or two after they closed up rolling around with him in their bed each night, Zak felt his absence keenly. It was becoming more and more obvious to Zak that he wanted Brody as part of their everyday lives, not just for the minutes or hours they could steal. But it was equally clear it wasn't going to happen on its own. Something was going to have to be done.

The fact that Brody always insisted on going home at the end of the night ate at Zak. He was trying to let the man come to them at his own speed, but it was hard to watch him walk away. And it had been harder again when Brody had said he wouldn't be joining them today.

Oh, Brody had been very apologetic. He'd said he wanted to join them. In fact, he'd said all the right things, even called this morning and explained that a family emergency meant he wouldn't be able to join them this evening either. It had all sounded very plausible, very reasonable. And it made Zak as nervous as hell.

Gradually, all the calm, relaxed feeling he'd managed to store up through the day – the store that was supposed to last him all week – drained away. Was Brody trying to edge away from them? Was he feeling smothered? Were they being demanding and clingy? Had asking Brody to join them on his day off been too much? Was he looking for a break from them already?

Zak forced himself to stop thinking about it. It was completely unproductive and it would give him an ulcer before he was thirty if he wasn't careful. Lark would never let him live it down.

Deep breath in. Deep breath out. Zak let the tension drain away from him again. He closed his eyes for a second and concentrated on the feeling of being connected to Lark and relaxed.

Settled again, Zak returned to his book, hoping to get another chapter or two read before they turned in for the night and letting his worries go for a few more hours of peace.

Then the doorbell rang with a drawn out, jarring insistence. Zak groaned wretchedly. Lark's grin only grew wider and Zak thought he might have even heard a tiny, evil chuckle escape the little shit's mouth.

Lark never answered the door, and Zak knew there was no way he was going to win no matter how hard be begged or complained or yelled. They'd been over that old ground for years and nothing was ever going to change.

With a loud, discontented grunt, Zak heaved himself up out of the lounge and stomped towards the front door.

Someone's ass better be on fire, he thought irritably as the buzzer sounded again, loud and far too long.

Lark just stretched out his legs and adjusted to make himself more comfortable. Smug bastard.

But the angry tirade he had been about to unleash on the poor unsuspecting sod on the other side of their door died in his throat. Zak was completely speechless as he was confronted with a bedraggled looking Brody, carrying a small, sleepy bundle protectively in his arms. When the light from the hall spilled out across the sleeping child, who appeared to Zak's uneducated eye to be about three or four years old, it stirred and began to whimper.

"Shh, Wolf. It's all right. Go back to sleep," Brody whispered.

Wolf! Zak stared in amazement at the pair. *What the* –

At the sound of Brody's voice the boy – Brody's brother? – settled and seemed to drift straight back off to sleep contentedly.

Brody's pale, strained face turned up to regard Zak with wide, tormented eyes. "I'm sorry. I just...I didn't have anywhere else to go."

Zak suddenly realised he could smell the heavy scent of smoke on Brody and the little boy. Smudges of ash dotted their faces and clothes.

"What the hell happened?" he asked, stepping back and ushering them inside when it finally registered that he was keeping them on the doorstep. "Come in. Come in."

"Thanks," Brody said, the weary, tight sound of his voice rubbing against Zak's senses.

"Brody? What are you –" Lark's questions cut off abruptly when he rounded the corner into the hall and finally caught sight of Brody and the boy. "What happened?"

"I...ah..." Brody looked increasingly lost and Zak suspected he was probably edging towards shock.

"Let's just get you two inside, huh? Then you can tell us what's going on." Zak hoped by keeping his voice even and firm and giving Brody clear direction he would be able to keep him calm and focused, too. It seemed to work. Brody walked steadily towards the living room.

"Are you okay? Are either of you hurt?" Lark asked, hovering anxiously at Brody's side and looking between him and the boy in his arms.

"No...I mean yes, we're fine. We managed to get out before..." Brody shivered. He didn't seem to know what to do with himself now that he was standing in the middle of the living room. He just stared around blankly.

"That boy doesn't look real big, but I bet he's getting heavy. You want me to take him?" Zak asked, reaching out to help, but Brody pulled away sharply.

"No!" He clutched the sleeping child tightly, but quickly eased his hold when the boy stirred restlessly against him. "It's fine. I just..."

Lark stepped up and laid his hand gently over Brody's forearm.

"It's okay, Brody. Why don't you take...Wolf?" Brody nodded, and Zak continued. "Why don't you take Wolf and go settle him down in the spare room?"

Brody nodded again and turned mechanically towards the bedrooms.

"Do you need a hand?" Zak was worried about the wooden, stilted way Brody was moving and his muted responses. He wasn't sure the man was fully functional right now.

"I'll be okay, I just..." Brody's voice trailed off as if he wasn't sure what he was at the moment.

"If you want you can take a shower in the en suite," Lark suggested.

Zak wasn't so sure Brody should be anywhere near slippery, wet surfaces right now, but he held back on saying anything when Brody nodded. Then again, it was quite possible Brody was just agreeing to everything right now because he couldn't muster any other reply.

"Thanks. I'll just…"

At least he was still responding.

"I'll leave a fresh towel and a change of clothes out for you. Come out when you're ready and you can tell us what's going on," Lark continued as if everything was fine and men turned up every day with boys in their arms smelling of smoke and in the early stages of shock.

"If you need anything—" Zak started to offer, but Brody cut him off.

"It's fine. I'll…thanks. I'll…I'll be back in a few…umm…I'll just settle Wolf in and then…"

"Take your time, Brody. We'll wait for you in the kitchen." With that Lark turned and started dragging Zak by the arm out of the living room.

And wasn't that a turn up for the books. Normally Zak was the one restraining Lark from going in guns blazing. But right now, Zak was fighting tooth and nail to resist jumping in and demanding to know what the hell was going on right now so that he could fix it. Then he could get on with telling Brody off for not sharing some very significant details with them. And obviously putting himself in danger if he was coming to them smelling of smoke and covered in soot.

Zak found himself feeling vaguely hurt, mostly confused and extremely frustrated. And he wasn't used to feeling any of those things. Worse still, he wasn't entirely convinced it was going to get better any time soon.

* * * *

Forty-five minutes later, Zak sat drumming his fingers on the countertop while Lark quietly sipped his coffee. This in itself was enough of a role reversal to freak Zak out. When the hell had Lark become the quiet, patient one?

They'd heard Brody use the shower about fifteen minutes ago, and Zak figured the man had about thirty seconds before he barged in to make sure Brody was all right.

"Why didn't he tell us about Wolf?" Zak demanded as he jumped up to begin pacing when his nerves couldn't take staying still anymore.

"He did, when we bumped into him downtown. We just—"

"That doesn't count and you know it."

"Hey! I was the one that wanted to follow him home and find out what was going on. You were the one that said to wait until he was ready to tell us."

"I didn't think he—"

Just when Zak was about to say something really stupid about something he knew absolutely nothing about, Brody stepped into the kitchen. Water droplets clung to his hair and eyelashes, or perhaps...no. Water droplets. Zak couldn't handle anything but water droplets right now.

"Is he asleep?" Lark asked, jumping up from his stool as Brody nodded. He went to fetch another mug from the cabinet. "You want coffee?"

Zak was relieved to see Lark was already pouring it before Brody answered. Obviously, Lark wasn't as calm and collected as he was making out. Which was a relief, because Zak felt about as far from either calm or collected as he could get. And he'd hate to be alone.

"Yeah. Yeah, that would be great." Brody fiddled with the sleeve of his sweatshirt. It was one of Zak's and hung long and loose on Brody's shorter, slighter frame.

"Sit down," Lark suggested as he poured the thick, rich coffee they preferred into Brody's mug and refilled his own. Zak declined a second cup; he was edgy enough as it was.

"Are you angry?" Brody blurted, not looking at either of them as Lark set a mug of coffee in front of him.

Brody looked incredibly young and vulnerable in that moment and Zak sighed. Was he angry? That was a tricky one. He was and he wasn't. It was more…

"Not angry, Brody, just—" Lark began, but Brody cut him off.

"Look, I understand if you don't want to get involved with someone who's raising a kid, but if you could just give us a couple of days to get—"

"Stop right there!" Zak's level of pissed off skyrocketed to new heights unexpectedly. "No one said anything about not wanting you, and we certainly won't be kicking you out. So you can get those thoughts out of your head right now."

"It was just a bit…" Lark, ever the peacemaker, tried to explain. But his voice trailed off again when it obviously became too much to try and contain in one sentence. "Why didn't you say anything? About Wolf? Is he really your brother, or is he—"

"Of course he's my brother." Brody bristled. Perhaps there was even more to Brody's story yet to come out.

Well, this time Zak wasn't prepared to wait until Brody was ready to give them answers.

"I just thought maybe he was your son or something," Lark continued quietly.

"Shit! Things would be so much easier if he was," Brody replied, bitterness and frustration lacing his voice as he let out a mirthless chuckle that had a suspiciously tight, hitching quality to it.

"How about you start at the beginning?" Zak suggested, staring down at the top of Brody's head, which was once again bowed over his coffee mug. He wouldn't look at either of them now.

"I have a better idea," Lark announced, reaching for Brody's hand and tugging gently until he stood up. "Why don't we all snuggle up on the couch and we can be comfy while Brody tells us his story."

It was obvious Lark wasn't going to be denied. They all trouped obediently in behind him. The coffee was abandoned in favour of cuddling together, with Brody sandwiched in the middle and Lark spreading a large afghan over all three of them on the couch.

"That's better," Lark announced, apparently happy now for the story to begin.

A long silence began to stretch out between them all. Zak was just wondering whether he was going to have to give Brody a nudge to get him to start, when he felt the man take a deep, shuddering breath.

"Do you know why my brother's called Wolf?"

Zak felt a little off kilter as Brody paused for a moment to collect his thoughts. Not quite the direction he had expected, but Zak shook his head anyway, willing to play along if Brody was starting to open up.

"It's because our mom was a mean bitch. She said Wolf's father—and God knows who that could have been—left her, and it was all Wolf's fault. She said

Wolf was bad luck. A wolf in sheep's clothing. A bloody greedy dog. She was always making some nasty little comment or snide remark. She said Wolf was...anyway, it's what she made them put on his birth certificate, so it's his name. And after a while it kind of stopped being a way for her to hurt us. It became something to be proud of. I never want him to feel bad about it. Wolf's a little fighter. He's seen more... Wolf's a good name now."

Brody began to pick at the afghan, but Zak didn't care. All his attention was focussed on the pain and tension radiating off their lover right now. Lark covered Brody's hand with his own and gave it a reassuring squeeze, which seemed to ease some of the stiffness in Brody's shoulders and help him carry on.

"Anyway, Wolf was about six weeks old when I met him. I was doing a..." Brody cleared his throat and hesitated, Zak knew whatever Brody had to say next wasn't going to be good, but he wanted to hear it anyway.

He wanted everything. No hiding anymore. Zak reached out and put his hand over Lark's, joining in to offer his support and encouragement.

Brody took another deep breath before ploughing on. "I was doing another stint in juvie when he was born. Shoplifting and..." Brody looked up at Zak with sad, frightened eyes, as if expecting disgust and rejection.

Zak suddenly had a pretty fair idea what was coming. "It's okay—"

"Soliciting," Brody said, his voice small but infinitely brave as he looked between them, meeting their eyes steadily—first Zak's then Lark's. "It wasn't the first time, but it was the last. When I turned eighteen, I got out and was probably about to end up doing more of the same, but then I found out about Wolf. I never turned a trick or stole or... I turned it all around. Ended up doing odd jobs whenever I could and...Yeah, I turned it all around after that."

Zak watched Brody straighten his shoulders.

"Wolf was the best thing that ever happened to me. Before him, I really...I just...once I knew, I just had to look after him, and I knew I had to get it together. I didn't want him to have to go through what I did. The best thing our mom ever did for either of us was to make me Wolf's legal guardian when I turned twenty-one."

Brody fiddled with a loose thread on the afghan, then chuckled without any real humour colouring his voice. "Hell of a twenty-first birthday present, huh? But I was so happy. She was dead six months later. It could have—" Brody shivered.

"How'd she die?" Lark asked softly.

"Drug overdose."

"I'm sorry," Zak said, not sure what else either of them could say in the face of such a terrible tale.

"Thanks, but...well...it was bound to happen. I'm just glad Wolf's too young to really understand or remember too much about it all. Before she went, I did my best to protect him from it."

"So you've been looking after Wolf all his life?"

"Yeah. It wasn't easy being around Mom and her addictions. She used Wolf to get what she wanted from me a lot, but at least she agreed to make me his guardian."

Lark reached up and turned Brody's face towards him. He leaned in for a long, sweet kiss.

"You're a good man, Brody McAllister," Lark whispered against Brody's lips, and Zak watched a deep blush tint the skin of Brody's cheeks a lovely hot pink.

Zak gently shifted Brody's face towards him, very aware the tale wasn't anywhere near finished yet. He softened his next question with a small kiss.

"What happened tonight?" Zak asked gently.

Brody looked away, the blush on his cheeks deepening to an almost impossible brick red. "When we moved here, I took a place over on fifth. Down by the dock."

Zak knew where Brody was talking about. While it wasn't the worst area, it had certainly seen better days.

"It was cheap and clean. Best of all, after we moved in we met Mrs. Tolimay. She's just the sweetest, most..." Brody cleared his throat again. "She agreed to babysit for me while I found work. It seemed like the most perfect, amazing stroke of luck. And it was. But last Monday — the night I had to cancel coming over — she had a funny turn. We took her to the hospital, but they weren't very helpful and by the time we got seen, she was fine again. I didn't... I mean she's getting on and all, but she really did seem fine, I swear she was. I would never have left Wolf with her if she hadn't been okay. Well...I mean she's a bit forgetful, but...I didn't think...she wouldn't hurt Wolf and I thought..."

Zak could see Brody beginning to edge towards panic. It seemed the whole thing had suddenly caught up with him with the realisation that Wolf might have been in danger. Zak wrapped his arms around Brody's trembling shoulders and pulled him in for a tight hug. He saw Lark snuggling closer and offering his comfort as well.

"Ssh. It's okay. Don't—"

"Oh, God! No it's not! This afternoon…I was just so tired. I only meant to rest my eyes, because Mrs. Tolimay had been acting a little more forgetful and spaced out than normal today, and I was getting worried, but…somehow she started a fire. I got us out okay, but… What if that had happened when I wasn't there? They might have both…Wolf could have —"

"Brody —"

"When we first started living with her I swear she was fine. In fact, she was great. But, I don't know, the last few days she just got really bad. I thought she was just forgetting to take her medication, so I made sure she got all her tablets on time and…she seemed okay again. I thought she was going to be fine. Then —"

"Wolf's okay, Brody. He's going to be just fine," Zak's firm, even voice didn't seem to be working to reassure him this time.

"I need to see him. I just…I need to see him breathing." Brody leapt up and ran out of the room.

* * * *

Zak held Lark against his side as they snuggled together in silence. Brody had been gone a long time now and in all probability wouldn't be back. Zak understood. Brody needed to be with his brother right now. He needed to be able to see for himself that Wolf was still alive and breathing. Then he needed to keep on looking to make sure he stayed that way.

It wasn't surprising. Zak knew he'd feel exactly the same way if Lark ever came that close to —

Zak caressed the arm Lark had draped loosely across him and refused to even think about it. He let the peace and quiet soothe him and allowed his mind to drift. Refusing to focus on anything in case his mind started to dwell on something he couldn't even handle in his imagination."

"Got room for one more?"

"Brody!" Zak struggled with Lark as they both rushed to sit up at the same time.

"Don't get up. I'd rather come to you." Brody quickly positioned himself back where he had been before he had hurried away to check on Wolf—right in between Lark and Zak, pressed up as close as possible to both of them.

"I didn't expect to see you again tonight." Zak watched Brody as he pulled the afghan back over them. He looked calmer. More relaxed and composed now.

Brody shrugged. "I couldn't settle."

Lark reached across and cupped Brody's cheek. "That's pretty understandable."

It was an innocent gesture—a gentle caress of comfort and support. But something changed in Brody's expression the moment Lark touched him. Passion and longing and desperate need flared to life in his eyes.

Brody lurched forward and took Lark's mouth in a hot, demanding kiss that was startling in its intensity. It went on and on until finally the two had to pull apart to catch their breath in shallow, panting gasps.

Before Zak could work out what to do, Lark pushed the afghan off their laps and straddled Brody's thighs.

"Lark..." Zak wasn't sure what he was going to say—maybe he would have asked whether this was such a good idea—but Lark ignored him anyway and Brody looked more than willing to do the same, so it didn't matter.

Taking Brody's face in his hands to hold him still, Lark leaned in and took possession of his lips.

Working steadily, he pushed the kiss deeper and worked his tongue in until soon they were moving and stroking across one another passionately. Moans of pleasure filled the room as Brody seemed to lose himself in Lark's mouth.

Perhaps this was just what Brody needed after all.

Reaching between his lovers, Zak carefully undid their buttons and zippers to free both their hard, leaking cocks while they continued to kiss and groan. Twisting to kneel on the couch, Zak reached in and wrapped his hands around both cocks. Sliding and working them together, he merged the pre-cum that wept freely from their slits, massaging it down their combined shafts in a slick, even coating.

When both Lark and Brody began to thrust towards each other and into Zak's hands, the trickle of pre-cum began to flow thicker and faster. Zak wriggled his way in between.

It was awkward as hell and only possible because both men where lean and flexible, but eventually Zak was able to lick the tips of the cocks in his hands. He bathed them repeatedly, relishing the sweet-salty taste that flowed over his tongue and the increasingly desperate sounds of the men above him.

Determined to get every last drop of the precious seed from them, Zak opened his mouth wide and did his best to take in the heads of both hard shafts at once. Stroking his tongue over and around their tips, Zak closed his eyes as the first hot spatters of cum washed over his tongue and hit the back of his throat. He swallowed around the cocks in his mouth awkwardly, lapping with his tongue to try to catch every drop. He wasn't sure who shot first, but soon they were both producing so much cum, no matter how hard he tried, some spilt out of his mouth and dribbled down his chin.

When the very last of the convulsive thrusts and jerks subsided, Zak pulled away to sit up. He closed his eyes as he savoured the moment. Suddenly, the couch shifted a little and he felt a tongue begin to lick at his chin and lips, cleaning off the last of the spilled cum.

When Zak felt someone begin to tug on his waistband and lower his sweatpants over his aching hard shaft, he lifted his hips to help and opened his eyes to pay attention.

Brody stared back at him. All his pain, self-recrimination, and fear were gone. Instead, there was hunger, and a passionate look Zak could see every day of his life and never get bored of. After one last lick of Zak's chin and a tiny smile, Brody lowered himself down beside Lark, who was already beginning to tease at Zak's foreskin — pushing and rimming it and tonguing the sensitive fold. Zak thrust forward to give them plenty of room to work, and Brody's tongue joined in the delicate, wonderful play.

Hot, wet mouths moved over him, joined to kiss, then pulled back to lick. Sharing Zak's cock between them, Lark and Brody worked at the long, thick shaft until Zak knew he couldn't last much longer. He gently ran his hands over both his beautiful lover's heads, feeling the silky smooth blond strands, so different, yet the same precious weight and feel, slipped through his fingers.

"Ahhhh! Oh! Gonna—" Zak tried to warn, but it was too late.

Ribbons of cum splashed out over their faces. Both of them diligently used their tongues to lick and catch the spray, or to clean each other until every last drop was caught and enjoyed.

Collapsing back against the arm of the couch, Zak spread his arms wide and invited Lark and Brody into his embrace. He gave a deep, contented sigh as they climbed up to rest against him.

"Thank you," Brody finally croaked.

Craning his neck with some difficulty, Zak managed to place a kiss on Brody's head, then turn and do the same to Lark.

Words that were too much to say right now, thoughts and feelings that were too fresh and raw to be spoken, bubbled up and tingled across Zak's lips. He wanted to say the words so badly he almost relented, but in the end he knew it wasn't time. Soon perhaps, once things were settled between them, but not right now. For now, Zak simply lay back and enjoyed the feeling of holding the two gorgeous men in his arms.

My gorgeous men, he reminded himself. All he had to do was convince Brody.

Chapter Ten

Barefoot, an apron protecting his best jeans and the pale blue T-shirt that emphasised his eyes, Lark whisked the pancake batter briskly and watched the creamy mixture swirl and coat the sides of the bowl with a smooth, even layer. *Perfect*. He swayed his hips from side to side in a little happy dance — congratulating himself on a job well done. Everything was just right.

He'd heard Brody and Wolf starting to move around about half an hour ago and set to work on making them a special breakfast straight away. By the time Brody had the little boy cleaned up and they emerged, everything would be ready to make them fresh, piping hot stacks of fluffy goodness.

Lark grinned. While he didn't know much about kids, Lark figured Wolf was likely to be starving after last night's adventure. And he really wanted them to feel welcome. Actually, he wanted them to feel like they had come home.

Lark had to admit he was a little nervous. He wasn't fooling himself. There was a lot riding on this morning. It could go either way right now, but he was determined to rig the dice with whatever means he had available, and they said the way to a man's heart was through his stomach. Personally, he thought maybe it was a little further south than that, but who was he to argue with conventional wisdom? And feeding the man's kid brother seemed like a pretty good idea, too.

Brody had needed to spend the night watching over Wolf. He had still been too stressed to do anything else, and Lark could understand that. But once Brody disappeared into the spare room, Lark and Zak had stayed up, talking and trying to work out their next move late into the night.

One thing was certain. Today, they all needed to have a good long talk about what came next. Lark felt like jogging on the spot and shaking out his limbs the way he'd seen professional runners do before a big race.

This was it. Time to put their cards on the table and see what happened.

Just as the butterflies started doing a little fandango in his stomach again, Lark glanced up to see Brody stepping into the kitchen, Wolf perched on his hip. The small, still slightly damp tow-haired boy turned wide, pale blue eyes on him, and Lark instantly saw the family resemblance. Brody and Wolf had the exact same, beautiful, intelligent eyes.

Lark watched as Wolf looked him over carefully, before focusing all his attention on the bowl where he continued to lazily stir the pancake mixture.

"Hi," Brody said, hefting the little boy a little higher on his hip.

"Good morning. How do you boys feel about pancakes and fruit for breakfast?" Lark asked, trying not to notice how uncertain Brody looked.

So many things needed to be sorted out. The tension sizzled and rode over Lark's skin. He just wanted to make it stop. Seeing Brody looking tense and unsettled in their home felt...wrong.

Why did everything have to be so complicated, anyway? In Lark's opinion, they didn't. Brody and Wolf needed a home; he and Zak had one. And that was it. But as usual, no one seemed to see how easy it could all be. Not the way he could.

"Umm...okay," Brody hedged.

Suddenly, the little boy's eyes drifted across the counter and came to rest on the bowls of fruit Lark had prepared.

"Brody," the little boy whispered in awe, "they got strawberries and the blue ones."

Lark chuckled. "You like blueberries and strawberries, huh?"

Wolf nodded enthusiastically, his eyes never leaving the glistening fruit.

"Want to help me get them ready?"

Wolf didn't seem to need any further invitation. He began to squirm and wiggle on Brody's hip, wanting to be put down.

Lark dragged a chair over to the sink then waited for Wolf to climb up before he filled a bowl with water and laid a hand towel on the drainer. He'd actually already washed the fruit, but he figured this would be a good way to break the ice.

"Here you go. You wash the strawberries off for me and then put them on the towel to dry. You think you can handle that?"

Wolf nodded, his little brow furrowing in concentration as he placed one large, ruby red strawberry in the bowl and watched it bob around. He carefully rolled it about so it was thoroughly washed all the way around.

Lark grinned at the little boy's diligence as Wolf placed the berry aside and reached for another. It looked like Wolf was going to be happily occupied for quite a while. At least until the pancakes were cooked, anyway.

"You better taste one to make sure they're okay, too," Lark suggested.

Wolf lunged at the washed berry and stuffed it in his mouth, grinning around the fruit. A trickle of juice dribbled down his chin before he licked it away.

"Make sure you leave enough room for pancakes."

"I will," Wolf replied brightly.

The little boy sounded completely relaxed and at home now, and Lark felt a wave of relief wash over him. He was going to like Wolf.

Turning back to start heating the pan for the pancakes, he saw Brody watching with a strange, slightly confused look on his face, as if he hadn't expected Wolf to be welcome in their home. And perhaps he hadn't. By the sounds of it, their own mother had pretty much rejected Wolf from birth.

Lark felt a spike of anger and protectiveness flare inside him. What sort of a person would abandon the bright, happy little child currently munching his way through the bowl of fruit at the sink?

"Thanks," Brody said quietly, his cheeks turning a little pink. "You...umm..."

Damn, the man looked even more uncomfortable now. Brody was obviously going to be a much harder sell than his brother. Lark racked his brain for the right thing to say. Maybe putting Brody to work was the answer with him, too.

"Could you ge—"

"Morning," Zak rumbled in a deep, sleepy voice as he padded into the kitchen.

Lark saw Brody tense and look over to where Wolf stood at the sink, industriously ploughing his way through the strawberries before he'd even vaguely washed them now. Wolf turned, his lips stained red with the berry juice and stared at Zak.

Lark felt his own muscles tighten. Zak was big. He was imposing. He was as soft and sweet as a toasted marshmallow, but with anyone that didn't know him, the first thought that probably crossed their mind was something along the lines of not wanting to bump into Zak in a dark alley.

Lark was just about to jump in to soothe the little boy, when Zak said, "Mmm! Those look good," pointing to the strawberry the little boy was holding. "Can I have one?"

Wolf calmly held out the berry and watched Zak walk over to take it out of his hand.

"Thank you." Biting into the fruit, Zak moaned theatrically. "Ooh! Yummy!"

"My name's Wolf," the little boy announced.

"Cool name. I'm Zak."

Wolf smiled and held out another berry.

"Yes, please." Once more Zak plucked the berry from the little boy's hand and popped it in his mouth.

Slowly, Lark felt himself relax. He wondered if it was some innate survival instinct that told the child Zak was safe. Or perhaps it was just that Brody had somehow—miraculously, given the circumstances—managed to do an absolutely amazing job of protecting and nurturing Wolf. He didn't seem the least bit insecure or intimidated by talking to the strange adults in a strange place.

Looking over, Lark saw Brody staring at Zak and Wolf as they continued to share the last of the strawberries.

"Mmm...smells like Lark's making pancakes," Zak said to the boy, reaching for another strawberry. "Do you like pancakes?"

"Oh yeah!" Wolf enthused as another berry disappeared into his mouth.

"Me too."

"If you guys will stop scarfing all the fruit and get the table set, we can all have some." Lark waved the spatula at the empty breakfast table, grinning when Zak and Wolf smiled around the last berries before getting to work.

For a moment, Brody didn't move. He looked too stunned to do anything but stare at them as they all moved around like it was part of some long established routine—Wolf setting out the plates and cutlery, Zak collecting cups and juice.

Lark felt the small cloud of doubt and uncertainty that had shadowed his mind lighten and drift away. He smiled over at Brody. This was going to work out. He just knew it was. And Brody would catch up soon.

"Come on, Brody. If you don't help you don't get any," Zak announced, handing Brody a jug of syrup.

"Can I have Brody's?" Wolf asked hopefully.

"Hey!" Brody cried, finally snapping out of his daze.

Lark chuckled and went back to flipping over the pancakes.

No, things weren't settled yet, but they'd get there. He was sure of it.

* * * *

Lark groaned. He'd eaten too many pancakes. Again. But once he'd started in on the stack he hadn't been able to stop. He loved pancakes. They were just so good.

"That was yummy," Wolf announced. "You're nearly as good at pancakes as Brody."

"Oh, really!" Lark said, straightening his shoulders and puffing out his chest as he pretended to be affronted by the very idea. "I think we're going to have to put your brother to the test on that one. I'll have you know I am the reigning pancake king."

Zak chuckled. "I can see a lot of pancakes in our future."

"Yay!" Wolf shouted, bouncing in his seat.

"I don't think I could look at another pancake again," Brody moaned, rubbing his stomach.

As the meal had progressed, with Wolf chattering away and pancakes filling their bellies, Brody had gradually relaxed. Now he looked almost as comfortable as his brother.

Lark breathed in and let a deep, contented smile form. He *knew* pancakes were the answer to everything.

"How about some TV time, Wolf? We need to clear up this mess and have a bit of a chat with your brother about some stuff," Zak said.

Before Zak had even finished the sentence, Lark could see the easy, relaxed zone Brody had found instantly disappear. He would have cursed if Zak hadn't been right. Damn it!

"Can I, Brody?" Wolf asked.

"Umm…sure." Brody looked across at Lark, doubt and uncertainty once again shadowing his eyes.

"Brody—" Lark started to reassure, but Zak interrupted.

"I'll be right back. Don't start without me."

Wolf bounced out of his chair and headed towards the living room with Zak following along behind him.

Looking over at Brody, Lark couldn't resist reaching out to take his hand. Brody looked so tense and worried right now. "It's going to be alright, Brody. We just need to—"

The sound of the TV coming to life cut Lark off. Within seconds, Zak came back into the room. Sitting at the table, he looked over at Brody, his face intense and serious now that Wolf was no longer present.

"I think the first thing I need to know is, do you want Wolf to know? About us, I mean." Zak leant back in his chair, crossing his arms and watching Brody closely. "I have to tell you, I don't do closets well, Brody. And Lark couldn't keep a secret to save his life."

"Hey!"

"Just telling it like it is, baby."

"I don't want you to have to change—" Brody began to say, but Zak stopped him.

"Brody, I'm not talking about just Lark and me. I mean all of us. I want you, Lark wants you, and you want us. And hiding it just isn't who we are. The question is are you going to be okay with that? What are you going to tell Wolf?"

Brody got up and began pacing around the room, not really looking at anyone and tugging on his lip pensively. Finally, he turned back to them.

"I'm not going to hide who I am from Wolf. I like you guys. I want to be with you. But Wolf needs stability right now. He needs—"

Lark jumped up and marched over to where Brody stood, stiff and tense and shifting anxiously as he struggled with everything they were laying out. Enough was enough.

One, if Brody couldn't handle them hugging and kissing while Wolf was awake, they needed to know that now. And two, they needed to stop with the bullshit and just get to the good bits.

Wrapping his arms around Brody, Lark leaned up and stole a brief, chaste kiss.

"So you stay here. Move in with us. We make the spare room Wolf's bedroom and you share our bed every night. Simple."

"I can't…"

"Stop," Lark demanded, barely resisting the urge to stomp his foot in frustration. "Do you love us?"

"What?" Brody looked genuinely shocked and a little panicky.

"Do you love us?" Lark reiterated, trapping Brody with his eyes so he couldn't hedge or look away.

"Lark, it's too soon," Zak started to say as he stepped towards them.

Lark turned on Zak, still holding on to Brody fiercely. "Do you want him to go? Could you stand it if Brody left? I want them to stay. I want—"

"Yes," Brody said.

"—them…What?" Lark looked back to Brody.

"Yes, I want to stay. Yes, I want to tell Wolf about us. Yes, I love you. Both of you. I know it's stupid and fast and—"

Lark sealed his lips over Brody to shut him up. He'd heard all he needed to know. The rest was just detail, and detail could be worked out as they went along.

Zak wrapped his arms around them both as they stood locked in each other's hold in the middle of the kitchen. Surrounded by dirty dishes, pots, and the sweet smell of warm maple syrup, Lark couldn't imagine a more perfect moment.

"You want to tell him about all of us? About being together?" Zak asked, a hint of uncertainty still lingering in his eyes.

Brody nodded. "Yes. And I want to stay with you. With both of you."

Stretching up, Brody placed a gentle kiss on Zak's lips and Lark's heart missed a beat. They were so beautiful together. Details would work themselves out.

Right now, Lark just wanted to bask in the lovely warm glow of sharing a precious moment and a brand new start with his men.

Chapter Eleven

Brody laid facing Lark, running his hands lazily along the smaller man's flank. He loved the soft, contented smile that played over his lover's lips and couldn't resist closing the distance between them to place a gentle, undemanding kiss there. One wasn't enough of course, so he did it again. Then a third time while he moved his wandering hand down to their cocks.

The three weeks since he and Wolf had moved in with Lark and Zak had been the best, most blissful and contented weeks Brody had ever known. He'd heard enough to know what a honeymoon phase was, but he didn't give a rat's ass. He was going to enjoy every wonderful moment without question.

Maybe Lark was rubbing off on him. Speaking of which...

Shuffling to reposition himself a little, Brody brought their cocks into alignment and gently touched the tips together. It felt lovely just to cradle the two shafts, still only half-hard as they both recovered from their recent lovemaking. But it wasn't enough. Brody wanted more. Very gently he began to manipulate Lark's foreskin.

"Mmm...I don't think I can," Lark mumbled as he nuzzled against the side of Brody's head and kissed his temple, before looking down between their bodies to where their cocks met and kissed.

Brody turned his head and placed his lips softly to Lark's forehead. "Shh. I just want to play a little."

Even though Brody was sure he wouldn't be able to muster another orgasm for a while either, he still wanted to share the intimate feeling of being connected to his lover. He had found he could never get enough—with Lark or Zak or all of them together. He always wanted more. He didn't want to waste a moment.

Slowly and carefully, he worked Lark's long foreskin over the head of his own cock until the two of them were locked together by the thin, sensitive fold of skin.

"Oh!" Lark breathed in awe, one trembling finger reaching down between them to trace along where they were now joined.

Brody couldn't believe how incredibly blessed he was to have found not one, but two uncircumcised lovers. Firstly, it was something he had never experienced with another lover. It made each and every time he stroked and caressed their cocks unique and therefore all the more special and intense for him. But more than that, the difference working that extra piece of flesh made to Zak and Lark's pleasure was astounding. And Brody had grown to love pleasuring the men. *His* men. They were so sensitive and responsive to his touch and he soaked in every moment of truly giving for the first time in his life.

When Lark looked back up at him, his eyes bright and curiously shiny in the early morning light, Brody's heart missed a beat—knowing he wasn't the only one affected. He leaned in and kissed Lark again, lingering over the sweet taste of his smaller lover.

"Love you," Brody whispered, still a little afraid of the words—as if saying them might make it all disappear somehow.

Lark smiled and kissed him back. "Love you, too."

Brody closed his eyes. His hand still supported their cocks where they rested together. He soaked in the amazing feeling of contentment and love he had somehow found and sighed happily. As the moments ticked by, Brody slowly let himself relax completely. It didn't get any better than this.

Except of course, Zak wasn't with them. He'd offered to take Wolf to preschool this morning so Brody and Lark could sleep in. The lazy morning start was pure heaven. Brody couldn't remember the last time he hadn't been forced to get straight up and look after Wolf, whether he was exhausted or not. And Zak would be home soon. Then their day off together could really get started.

"Thank you for finding Wolf a place in the preschool programme. He's having so much fun. I just...I can't believe how good you and Zak have been to us."

Lark kissed him again.

"You don't have to thank us. It's our pleasure. Really."

"I still don't feel right about you paying—"

Lark leant forwards and cut him off as he sealed their mouths together for a deep, intense kiss. The movement shifted their cocks and Brody felt Lark slip away from him, but the kiss and the hand that began to stroke over his back and shoulders did a lot to soothe his disappointment.

"Hush. No more of that," Lark whispered.

Lark's voice was husky with sleep and recent passion, but there was no arguing with him when he was like this. Brody already knew enough not to bother even trying.

As they settled back down to lie together contentedly, Brody heard keys rattling and the locks at the front door tumble. Zak. A wicked, happy smile pulled at Brody's lips as he considered the possibilities with Wolf safely off at preschool for the day.

"Lark!" Zak bellowed as the door closed with a heavy thud.

Lark rolled his eyes theatrically as he grinned over at Brody, who couldn't help grinning back.

What had the little troublemaker been up to this time? Brody wondered as he watched Lark climb from the bed with a much put upon look on his face.

"Larry Kenneth Piper! Get your ass out here right now!"

Lark froze, his eyes going wide then narrowing in displeasure. "Unless you plan on those words being listed as the primary suspect in your murder, you take that back right now Zakariah James!" he shouted back at Zak, heading towards the door in full high dudgeon.

"Larry?" Brody asked, fighting a chuckle.

Lark turned the frown on him. "You shut up. You didn't hear that."

Brody's smile got even wider. Oh, man! This was priceless ammunition and they both knew it. He planned on keeping Lark's real name carefully filed away for maximum effectiveness the next time the smaller man started to get out of hand.

Lark walked away, his proud, regal air of dismissal somewhat lost because he was stark naked. As he stalked off, he just looked too amazingly cute to be taken seriously.

But Brody didn't get a chance to bask in the knowledge that he had a way to rib the little troublemaker for long. As he settled back into the warm, soft mattress, Brody heard Zak start yelling.

"What the hell is this?" Zak demanded angrily.

"Oh, Fuck! I can explain, Zak. I swear."

Oh, shit, he really is angry! Brody leapt out of bed.

As Brody ran in, he skidded to a halt and eyed the two men facing off across the room with alarm—Zak looking more furious than Brody had ever imagined the man capable of. And Lark looked as white as a ghost as he stared at the letter and envelope in Zak's hand as if it were a snake about to strike out and bite him.

"Oh, I can't wait for you to try. What the fuck is this, Lark?" Zak yelled again, holding up the sheet of paper and waving it around angrily. "How long have you been hiding this?"

"It's not like that! I was dealing with it. I knew how you'd react. I didn't want to make a big deal out of it."

"Didn't want to make a big deal out of it!" Zak's face turned an even angrier shade of red as he spun around and paced away, obviously struggling against a truly incandescent explosion of pent-up rage.

Brody watched as Zak took a deep breath and turned around to face them once more. "This guy's been threatening you. What the hell is there not to make a big deal about?"

"What's going on?" Brody asked, confused and a little frightened by the way the pair were yelling at one another. It brought back some very unpleasant memories. Memories that twisted his gut with tension, making him nauseated to the point of wanting to throw up.

"We can't afford the negative publicity," Lark explained in a voice rising to meet Zak head on. "You'd have wanted to get the police involved. Which would have meant the media. It would have been a nightmare."

Brody looked over at Zak, remembering the man saying something along the same lines when the back of the house area had been messed up by a vandal. But Zak was completely oblivious, and Brody still didn't really know what the hell was going on.

"How can you worry about a thing like that when this...person is sending you threatening letters?" Zak cried, his voice increasing in volume with his obvious agitation.

"Would someone tell me what's going on?" Brody demanded.

"And I'll tell you what's a nightmare!" Zak bellowed at Lark, completely ignoring Brody as he stalked over to confront their smaller lover. "It's knowing that this crackpot's been after you and you didn't even bother to tell us!"

"Calm down, Zak," Brody pleaded, interrupting before Lark could let fly with another retort.

"Did you know about this?" Zak yelled, turning on Brody suddenly.

"No! I don't even know what you're talking about!" Brody said, needing all his courage just to stand his ground against the angry man when his natural instinct was to run for the hills.

"Don't yell at him!" Lark shouted at Zak.

Brody would have been grateful for Lark coming to his defence if it hadn't been for the yelling.

"Just stop it. Both of you! Stop it!" Brody cried, hating himself when he couldn't prevent his hands from coming up to cover his ears or the fearful step he took away from them both.

He hated the panic – the overwhelming need to run he felt whenever people raised their voices or started fighting around him. He couldn't handle conflict or even disagreements. He just wanted them to stop. All the peace and contentment he had felt a few minutes ago disappeared, like smoke in a raging storm.

"Brody..." As Zak reached out for him, Brody flinched automatically.

Fuck.

Zak looked as if he'd been sucker punched.

"Sorry," Brody murmured in apology, looking down at his bare feet as his face heated with embarrassment.

"It's okay, Brody." Lark cautiously stepped forward and very slowly wrapped his arm around Brody's waist, snuggling into his side. "I'm the one that's sorry." Lark turned his head back to Zak. "Can we please get dressed and talk about this, Zak? I'm sorry, okay? I fucked up."

Brody risked looking over at Zak. He stood rooted to the spot, staring at them cuddled together. Brody felt a tremor of trepidation chase over his skin.

"Brody, I didn't...I wouldn't..." Zak sounded lost and miserable, but worst of all he sounded hurt.

Now Brody felt even more wretched than he had when the yelling had overwhelmed him. "It's all right. I just...I don't do well with yelling." And wasn't that the understatement of the fucking century.

Lark tugged on his arm, leading him back to the bedroom. "Clothes. And then...I...I think we need to talk."

Brody didn't think he'd ever heard Lark sound quite so subdued and forlorn.

Oh, fuck. He really had screwed it all up somehow. *Stupid fear. Dumb ass can't handle a bit of yelling, fucking baby.* Brody chastised himself even as the terror began to ride him hard. Couldn't they just go back to the start of the morning? To the snuggling and cock-docking? How had everything gone so wrong when it had all been going so right for once?

* * * *

Ten minutes later, Brody walked back into the living room. A loose, casual T-shirt and sweatpants made him feel slightly less exposed. Unfortunately, his emotions and the tension strumming through the room were still too raw for him to feel comfortable.

Zak was sitting on the edge of the couch. He still looked angry. The knots in Brody's gut tightened when Zak glanced up, then quickly turned away with a sad, guilty look on his face.

Fuck. Not even a month and he'd fucked it all up with one stupid, cowardly automatic reaction. Brody wrapped his arms protectively around his middle and tried focusing on Lark to distract himself from his mounting panic.

Lark was spreading a sheaf of papers out on the coffee table. After adding the letter from today, he sat back on his haunches on the floor beside the couch. Brody knew the instant Lark spotted him standing in the doorway, because a sad expression came over his face.

"I'm sorry," Lark murmured. "This isn't how I wanted to spend the day."

"Me either." Zak shifted in his spot and ran his hand over his head.

At least everyone seemed calmer now, if still tense and uneasy. Brody breathed a sigh of relief. He could handle tense and uneasy. Just not yelling.

"Can someone just please explain what's going on?"

The longer the silence continued, the more Brody found himself getting both agitated and slightly irritated with not knowing what had caused the men he loved to start fighting so suddenly.

"I've been getting letters," Lark finally said.

"Threatening letters," Zak growled.

"They didn't start off that way but...yeah. Look, let me just show you."

Reaching over, Lark picked up one sheet from the pile and held it out.

"This was the first one. Basically it's a very long-winded 'you're sick, you need to get help'. It arrived the day after Gus quit."

Brody read a little of the opinionated, hateful letter when it was passed over to him. It certainly wasn't light or fun reading, but there was nothing truly sinister about it. He still wished Lark hadn't tried to cope with it on his own.

"I kept it, but I pretty much hoped it was a one-off rant and tried to forget about it." Lark picked up two more letters. "These two are basically the same, but by the fourth...well, it does sound more threatening. Not vicious, but... I called in a local investigator and had him try to trace the letters back to whoever sent them."

"You did what?" Zak looked shocked, and Brody couldn't blame him.

Telling strangers the story, showing them the progressively more abusive letters, Brody wasn't sure he liked the idea himself.

"I brought in professionals." Lark's voice was tight and defensive; it was obvious this hadn't been an easy decision for him to make, but it was one he was going to stand by. "I thought if I could find out who it was that was sending the letters I could go and confront them. Tell them to leave us alone. Make them stop somehow. I don't know…something. But it was no use. There was nothing traceable and no leads."

"But it has to be Gus. Doesn't it?" Brody suggested, surprised that Lark didn't agree immediately.

"No," Lark said, shaking his head.

"What do you mean, no? He's the bastard that started all this!"

"Yeah, but I had the investigators check. He's not even in the state. He's gone back to live with his sister in Seattle, and these are all local postmarks. So it's someone around here."

Brody looked between his lovers in confusion. "So there's someone else in the kitchen determined to…"

"Maybe someone said something to someone else. We can't assume anything." Zak stood up and paced towards the window.

Brody took a deep breath and slowly let it out. It was time to get everything out in the open, but he didn't relish the next few minutes. "Do you think the person who wrote the letters did the paint attack as well?"

"What paint attack?" Lark asked, his voice rising in alarm and confusion.

"Brody…"

Brody ignored Zak's rumbling censure. "Someone wrote," he hesitated a moment as he looked over at a dark and brooding Zak and swallowed before he continued, "they wrote 'YOU SICK FREAKS!' and threw paint at the back of the restaurant the day after Gus said all those things in the kitchen."

Lark turned on Zak in disbelief. "And you had the balls to go off at me!"

"One stupid message scrawled in paint on a building is not the same as multiple personal letters escalating to threats of unknown consequences."

"Only two of the letter before today sounded anything like a threat. And I was dealing with it!" Lark shot back.

Zak picked up the last letter and waved it about in evidence. "This is not just some idle threat! It made my blood run cold when I saw it. 'You were warned' and 'Now face the consequences'. Fuck, Lark! This is serious."

"Please," Brody whimpered, trying to hold it together as the voices rose again to border on yelling.

Instantly, the pair froze.

"Sorry," Lark murmured in apology.

Brody couldn't leave it like this. He knew he had to explain, but he didn't want to. He didn't want to think about it, to dredge up the past and think about what had happened to him as a child. And he really didn't want to have to say the words and tell Zak and Lark about it. Brody scuffed his bare toes against the thick carpet pile and tried to get out just enough.

"Always they would yell. Mom and her boyfriends. Sometimes they would hit me. Sometimes they'd just tell me to go away. Most of the time they would be too drugged out of their minds to care. But always there was the yelling. I just...I can't stand it now. You know?"

Lark moved closer and wrapped his arms around Brody, leaning into him.

Zak looked over at them for a long, pregnant moment and Brody found he couldn't look away from the intense, pale green-brown eyes.

"Come here." Zak's gentle, firm command did funny things to Brody's insides, and he found himself moving without consciously making the decision to obey.

When he was within arm's reach, Zak slowly, carefully pulled Brody in against his chest. Then Lark stepped up behind him and Brody found himself sheltered and surrounded by the two of them.

"I'm sorry we started yelling again, Brody. You know we'd never hurt you, don't you?"

Brody turned his head and concentrated on the strong, steady heartbeat beneath his ear. He was glad he didn't have to meet Zak's intense, penetrating gaze. He knew Zak wouldn't hurt him — at least, intellectually he did, but —

"I'd never, ever hurt Lark either. I'm just angry that he didn't tell us about this."

Lark's forehead came to rest between Brody's shoulder blades and he felt the smaller man heave a heavy sigh against his back.

"I'm so, so sorry. I thought I was doing the right thing," Lark said softly.

Zak reached around and ran his large hand over Lark's hair. Brody leaned into Zak and just breathed for a few moments, soaking in the warmth and connection between the three of them. He tried to focus on that and push everything else out.

"I'm sorry, too," Zak whispered, leaning his cheek on the top of Brody's head.

For a long time the three of them clung together, letting peace steal back into the room. No one spoke.

Everyone concentrated only on breathing and holding on.

"I think we need to discuss this with Wolf, too," Zak eventually said.

"What?" Brody jerked back, not sure he had heard correctly. They couldn't talk about this sort of thing with a four year old. Wolf just wouldn't understand. Brody didn't understand, how the hell was Wolf supposed to cope with it all?

"Not all of it, Brody," Zak clarified, "but I think he should know that there are people out there that might not like us. People that might want to...hurt us. We don't have to tell him how. We could just explain that these letters hurt us in a way. And that there might be other ways they...might try to hurt us. Let's just make him aware, okay?"

"You don't think...?"

"No, Brody. Nothing is going to hurt that little boy. Nothing. I won't let it. I won't let anyone hurt you or Lark either. Wolf's safe here. And so are you and Lark."

Brody wanted to believe. He really did, but doubt lingered and niggled at the back of his mind.

"I want to talk to this investigator." Zak shifted his hold so that Lark could move under one arm while Brody snuggled into the opposite shoulder.

"We need to tell them about your paint incident, too," Lark replied.

Brody tensed, readying himself for the conversation to deteriorate into another argument. But Zak simply squeezed him gently.

"It's okay, Brody. We're not going to fight anymore. It's pointless. We need to stick together and sort this mess out. Not fight amongst ourselves."

"I like that idea. Sticking together," Brody murmured.

"Mmmm...me too," Lark stretched across Zak's body and cupped Brody's cheek before leaning in for a soft, slow kiss. "Sticking together sounds good. I hate fighting with Zak, but the make-up sex...oh, baby!"

Brody felt so strange when a small, strangled little chuckle managed to escape him. The way he had been feeling only a few minutes ago he didn't think he'd be capable of it. But Lark always seemed to be able to make him smile. Brody's grin stretched even wider when Zak gently jostled Lark's shoulder and pulled him in for a tight, one armed hug against his side.

"Behave, Trouble," he warned playfully.

"Never!" Lark sounded truly affronted by the suggestion, and Brody laughed again.

Lark placed a light, tender kiss against Brody's lips.

"Love you," he whispered, before turning his head up to Zak and treating him to the same gentle affection. "Love you, too."

"Love you, Lark," Zak and Brody managed to echo in unison and Brody felt something ease inside him.

It was going to be okay. Really it was. Lark and Zak wouldn't let it be anything else but okay. And Brody was determined to hold on to what they had. Fiercely, with both hands.

Whoever was doing this to his men could just fuck off. Brody had found something good. Something wonderful and strong. He wasn't giving it up for anyone, especially not to some small-minded, arrogant asshole who was so cowardly he had to leave anonymous hate mail rather than just come out and say what he had to say face to face.

Chapter Twelve

Brody finished sweeping the entryway and straightened the kink in his back. The twenty-four hours since Lark had come clean about the letter, and Zak about the vandalism, had been pretty tough. Explaining the situation to Wolf without frightening him had been hard work, but Brody was glad Zak had insisted. He felt better knowing his brother wasn't completely unaware. Brody hoped it made Wolf less vulnerable this way. Just in case.

Settling back into their normally peaceful domestic relationships and routine had been a little tricky at first, too. But Brody had to admit the make-up sex was fantastic. He was stiff and sore in places he never knew he had. It was such a pity they all had to work later on today. He had much more creative things he'd rather be doing with his lovers this evening, but the real world was intruding.

He would be looking after Wolf through the afternoon until around six, then Zak would come to relieve him so he could help out in the kitchen until close. Hopefully, after that there would be time to find more soft, vulnerable spots to mess with before they all fell asleep in a tangled heap together.

Just as Brody began to grin like an idiot and turned to go find someone to share his happy mood with, the front door bell chimed. He placed the dustpan on the small hall table and leaned the broom beside it, then opened the door – and froze in horror.

"Good morning. I'm Officer Rosenthal and this is Officer Denkewitz. We're looking for Zak and Larry Piper."

Brody felt his heart leaping about in his throat and swallowed heavily to try and get the organ to settle down. Flashbacks of Leonard's smug face, police officers' sneering comments and the crowded, hostile courts that had sentenced him to juvie battered for space in his mind. They jostled and pressed in on him, threatening to send him down into a sea of madness.

"Is there a Zak or Larry Piper living here?"

Brody nodded, too afraid to speak and possibly betray himself or his lovers somehow.

"Are they at home?" Officer Denkewitz asked, speaking to him as if he was a rather slow child.

Brody didn't care. He nodded silently in reply. Maybe they'd leave if they thought he couldn't string two words together.

"May we speak with them?" the first officer hinted.

No such luck, obviously.

"Perhaps if we could come inside for a moment?" Denkewitz suggested pleasantly.

Brody froze. He didn't want to. He really didn't want to let the two imposing men in uniform into the house. He felt the threat of their presence like a physical force battering at him.

Just as they looked like they were going to become insistent, Brody felt Zak step up behind him. He knew it was Zak. He could feel the solid presence and heat from his larger body seeping into him even though he couldn't tear his eyes away from the men at the door. He wanted to lean back into it, have Zak wrap his arms around him and tell the cops to go away. But he didn't. He just stood staring at the two policemen on their doorstep.

Zak, in contrast, didn't hesitate. He gently took the door out of Brody's hand and pushed it open wide.

"I'm Zak Piper. Please come in, gentlemen."

Brody snapped his head around to stare at Zak in slack-jawed disbelief. He felt himself being gently pulled away from the door to let the stranger inside.

"We were just about to have coffee. Would you care for some, gentlemen?"

As Zak led the men down the hall towards the kitchen, Brody had to rush to catch up. Fear prickled all over his body. He felt every hair stand on end and a fine sweat break out across his skin.

Stepping out of the short hall from the front door, Brody saw Lark look over and jump up from the couch where he had been reading a magazine. Lark's reaction only made Brody's own sense of foreboding worse.

"Lark, get the file, please?" Zak asked calmly.

When Lark scurried off without a word, Brody's heart started to truly pound. He could feel himself edging towards a panic attack as Zak led them all into the kitchen. What was going on? Why were the police here?

Just as Lark returned holding a slim folder of paperwork, Wolf came running into the kitchen. He skidded around the bench and barrelled towards

Brody in his usual energetic display of affection. Aiming to tackle-hug Brody's knees, he froze when he saw the police officers.

Lifting up his arms with a suddenly serious look on his face, Wolf silently demanded to be picked up. He waited until Brody held him securely in his arms before returning his gaze to the police.

"Who's that?" he asked, pointing at the officers standing on the far side of the counter.

"This is Officer...I'm sorry I don't know your names," Zak said politely.

It was all so calm and controlled. Brody was immensely glad Zak had taken charge of the situation. He wasn't sure he would be able to speak at the moment to save himself.

"Rosenthal and Denkewitz," one of the officers supplied, staring at Wolf.

Brody tightened his hold on his brother, consciously having to fight to relax his grip around the boy. "They've come to say hello," he suggested in a thin, reedy voice he hardly recognised.

Zak looked over at him strangely. But there was no way Brody was going to let Wolf become afraid of cops. Brody was afraid enough for both of them. His experience had never been good when it can to police officers and the law. Brody felt his palms begin to tickle and sweat. But Wolf shouldn't be scared of them.

But what if they were here to investigate how he was caring for Wolf? Maybe they had heard about the fire? Or maybe they wanted to know why he had left Wolf with Mrs. Tolimay. Or...or perhaps...Brody's heart pounded impossibly hard against his ribs and he felt lightheaded with fear. He could lose Wolf.

Brody fought for control. He couldn't let the little boy know that he could be taken away. Brody breathed in and out and tried to project a calm, serene appearance, if only for Wolf's sake. The cops would have to shoot him before he let them take Wolf away, he decided.

Don't look afraid, Brody reminded himself. *Cops always thought you were guilty if you looked afraid.*

"Are you going to find the bad people that keep hurting my brother and his friends?" Wolf demanded.

"Umm…" one of the officers began uncertainly.

"Good!" Wolf barrelled on, completely oblivious to any other possibility. "Cause hurting people and making them feel bad isn't right. They shouldn't be allowed any ice cream. Brody said if you're naughty you don't get ice cream."

"It is bad," Officer Denkewitz confirmed grimly. "Does anyone ever hurt you?"

Zak's face instantly turned as dark as a late summer thunderstorm, and it was obvious he was about to explode. All traces of reasonable, composed man evaporated. Fortunately, Wolf saved the day.

"No," he said with blithe innocence. "Brody wouldn't let them, and Zak and Lark are looking after us now, too, so no one gets to hurt me." Apparently finished with the officers, Wolf turned to Brody. "I'm hungry. Can I have a cookie?"

"How about a sandwich and a drink of milk?" Lark suggested, and Brody was so relieved he'd have to remember to kiss the man next time they were alone.

He didn't think he'd be able to sound anything but hysterical right now.

"Okay," Wolf replied reluctantly looking disappointed before his face suddenly brightened. "Can I have a cookie if I eat all my sandwich?"

Lark chuckled and Zak grinned, his face still tight with anger, but the tension in the room beginning to unexpectedly lighten under the boy's sunny, carefree disposition. Even Brody felt a tiny smile tug at his lips. He was still as nervous as hell with the police officers in the room, but Wolf's happy influence was hard to resist.

"Deal, squirt. But crusts and all," Brody managed to croak out.

"Okay!" Wolf wiggled excitedly to get down and raced to the fridge.

"We have a few questions we'd like to ask you —"

"Perhaps down at the station," Officer Rosenthal said as he eyed Wolf pointedly.

Brody felt the air rush in and out of his lungs in great panicky gulps. They were taking Zak and Lark away.

"No —"

"Brody," Zak said firmly, moving to stand in front of him and gripping his shoulders with just enough pressure to get his attention. "It's going to be fine. We're just going to go down to the police station, sort this out and be right back." Zak reached into his pocket and pulled out his wallet. After a quick search he handed Brody a small white business card. "I want you to call this number. It's our lawyer, Mac. Have him meet us down there. Can you do that?"

Brody clutched the card like a lifeline and nodded as he stared up at Zak. He was too terrified to take his eyes off the man in case it was the last time he ever saw him. As he felt Lark move past him, Brody wanted to reach out and grab him so he wouldn't leave. Then he felt a small hand settle into his own.

Looking down, Brody saw Wolf watching him, his thumb in his mouth in a gesture that only emerged now when Wolf was feeling sick or tired...or anxious. Brody struggled to put a weak smile on his face and squeezed Wolf's little hand gently.

"Back soon, guys," Lark called cheerfully as he left the room.

Brody wasn't sure who he was trying to reassure, but it did nothing to ease the tight tangle of cold, hard knots that had formed in *his* stomach. The knots pulled even tighter now that he could no longer see his lovers, and threatened to double him over when he heard the front door close behind them.

He wanted to run out, drag them back inside and lock the world, and more specifically the policemen, out. He wanted to pull his men under the covers of the bed and make it all go away. But instead, he bent down and picked Wolf up, giving him a quick, thorough hug.

"How about that sandwich? Then I might even be able to find a couple of choccy-chip cookies. One for you and one for me, huh? I think we deserve it."

Wolf smiled and nodded enthusiastically around his thumb.

"Come on then. You can help." Brody thought they could both use the distraction of work and chocolate.

But it still promised to be a long, torturous afternoon.

* * * *

Brody paced and fussed. He checked the window to see if he could spot Zak and Lark coming back, and he waited. Impatiently.

Fuck! Fuck! Fuckity! Fuck! What the hell was going on? The lawyer, Mac something or other, had said maybe a couple of hours. It had been four now. He'd had to call Rio, Mark—the new mains chef—and the senior waitress in early to handle getting the restaurant prepped and opened up for dinner. He couldn't leave Wolf, and he had no idea when Zak and Lark would get back. So all he could do now was cool his heels and wait.

Shit! Shit! Shit! Brody yanked on his hair and growled in frustration. He couldn't even go down and see what was happening at the police station. Wolf had finally settled down for an afternoon nap. He'd been unsettled and stirred up all afternoon, but had finally fallen asleep about thirty minutes ago. And there was no way he was taking his little brother to a crowded, noisy, smelly police station, anyway.

Suddenly, Brody heard the key in the lock. Racing madly to the front door, he was just in time to see Zak securing the latch quietly behind them and a weary-looking Lark hanging up his coat. Flying across the short space that separated them, Brody flung his arms around the pair and pulled them into a tight hug, burrowing his head between them and breathing in their combined scents.

"What happened?" he asked, not the slightest bit ashamed of the way his voice quivered. He was just too damn glad to have them back home and in his arms.

He had begun to imagine all sorts of horrible scenes. Everything from social services turning up to take Wolf away right then and there, to having to see Zak and Lark paraded before a jury in handcuffs, to the cops banging down the door to arrest him, too.

Zak stroked his hand down Brody's back and pushed gently at his shoulder. "Come sit down," he commanded.

"What did they want? Were you charged with anything? Are they coming back?" Brody asked, ignoring Zak's attempt to calm him down.

Zak sighed, then took Brody and Lark's hands and dragged them to the couch. He pulled them both down so they rested on either side of him and wrapped an arm around each of their shoulders, snuggling them in tight to his body.

Brody really was starting to panic now. This couldn't be good. "What the hell's going on?" he demanded, the stress and strain eating away at him like acid.

"It's okay, Brody. We're fine," Lark tried to reassure him.

But Brody still couldn't stop the shaking as he waited for Zak to say something.

"An anonymous caller rang and made allegations of incest against us," Zak finally admitted.

Zak instantly released Lark and used both arms to grab hold of Brody's waist as he tried to jump up and run to collect Wolf so they could all high-tail it out of town. He held on and gently but firmly pulled Brody back down into his lap.

"It's fine, Brody. It's all sorted. We're not going anywhere. They're not coming to take Wolf away from you. He's safe. You're safe."

Brody ignored him as he struggled furiously. "How can you say that? They're going to come back. Incest...it's illegal," he hissed, but finally stilled when it became apparent Zak wasn't going to let him go and there was no way he was going to break out of Zak's huge, muscular arms.

Brody didn't care about the incest. It wasn't even something he really thought about anymore. But others did. The law did. And Brody couldn't do anything about that. The only thing he could do was keep Wolf safe from the system, one way or another.

"Brody! It's fine. Really." Zak tried to say as Brody started struggling against him again. Just thinking about Wolf being taken away—

"Brody! We're not actually brothers," Lark said.

Brody froze and stared over at Lark. What the fuck?

Zak growled ominously, and Brody saw Lark roll his eyes.

"Okay! We're not blood brothers. Is that better, grumble bum?" Lark asked, poking Zak in the side.

"What?" Brody interrupted before Zak could start up the tirade he could clearly see the man about to launch into. "I don't understand."

"I mean we're brothers, but only by marriage. His dad married my mom," Lark explained, rudely jabbing a finger into Zak again, then quickly snatching it back when Zak made a grab for it.

"And you didn't think to mention this?" Brody demanded, his blood pressure soaring. How could they have…?

"You said it didn't matter," Zak pointed out.

"And I did try to tell you," Lark added, far too reasonably for Brody's scrambled, very unreasonable brain.

"When?" Brody demanded, looking between the two calm men in disbelief.

"On that Tuesday after Gus had his little hissy fit at our expense," Lark replied casually.

Brody tried to think back, but the exact conversation eluded him. He'd have to take Lark's word for it. But really, that was hardly the point.

"But why would you…? I mean why didn't you just sort everyone out and explain it to them?"

"Because it's none of their fucking business!" Zak snapped. "Lark is my brother, plain and simple. I don't give a flying fuck what people think about me loving my brother with all my heart! It's their problem, not mine! And no one ever fucking believes us anyway."

Lark sighed and gently stroked Zak's arm, petting and soothing the agitated man. Brody just continued to stare. Lost and not sure which way was up anymore, Brody shook his head in disbelief. The whole situation had turned on its head. The vandalism, the letter…the police. It had all been —

"Zak refuses to call anyone but my mother Mom," Lark explained.

"She was my mom. The bitch that gave birth to me was just an egg donor. I won't degrade my memory of Lynn just because some asshole has a problem with who I choose to sleep with."

"Zak's —" Lark looked over to Zak. Whatever Lark had been about to say, he corrected mid-sentence. "Zak's egg donor walked out on him and his dad when he was seven. I think both of them wished she'd gone a lot sooner than that. She wasn't really the…mothering type."

"She wasn't even the sane type," Zak growled.

"My mom…yeah, Mom was there for Zak and his dad. That's how our parents got together."

"But why not just —"

Lark interrupted him, "This isn't the first time this sort of thing has happened to us. The last time —"

"The last time, Lark and I ended up finishing college six states away from home because no one wanted to listen or believe us. This place was a new start for Mom and Dad, and it was a new start for us. But I refuse to be run out like that again. Especially when we're not doing anything wrong. Now that Mom and Dad have..." Zak swallowed. "We're not doing anything wrong or illegal by any definition now."

"That's why you were so angry when Lark didn't tell you about the letters. Why you wanted to hide the vandalism." Finally, the last pieces began to fall into place for Brody.

Zak nodded. "Yeah. After the paint, I kept a really close eye out for anything, but when it just faded away, I wanted to let it go. I hoped it was all over. Then the letters and thinking Lark was in danger..."

"I thought I could handle it and not have you getting all upset." Lark leaned in to rest his bowed head against Zak shoulder, looking contrite and solemn.

"I hated it, Lark. It hurt thinking you'd hidden something like that from me. That you could have been in danger and didn't want me to help."

"I'm sorry," Lark muttered.

Brody stared at the two of them. Zak was the fixer. He wanted to make this all go away. And, crazy as it might sound, Lark was the protector. He wanted to protect Zak, no matter what. It was a strange and oddly touching underlying dynamic in their relationship.

Brody still found it difficult to comprehend why the two men would put themselves through all the hardships and torment that the nature of their relationship caused them. But at the same time, he had to admire them. They loved each other no matter what. Nothing had broken them. No matter how vicious or malicious the attack on them had been.

"So, do you think this is what they meant when they said 'you were warned' in that last letter? You think this was the consequences, calling the cops?" Brody held his breath and hoped.

"Yeah. I think so," Zak said, easing back into the couch with Brody still perched on his lap and resettling his arm around Lark so they were all cuddled together again.

"So, what now?" Brody asked. He still couldn't find it in him to relax. Every part of him still felt tense and ready for the next attack.

"So, now we cuddle and ignore the bastard," Zak announced. "We've—"

"What?" Brody's voice was high and incredulous again. "How can you—?"

"I won't let them win," Zak explained. "I won't let them mess up what we have."

Brody stared at Zak, taking in the completely serious, determined look on his face.

"I'm with Zak," Lark added. "I just want to love on you both and forget about them."

"But—"

Lark cut Brody off by taking his lips in a fierce, demanding kiss.

The kiss dragged on and Lark continued to thrust his tongue into Brody's mouth, impatiently entering and claiming every part with a hungry insistence. Slowly, Lark repositioned himself until he was on his knees on the couch. Then he toppled Brody back into the soft cushions. Brody's legs pinned Zak down, but he couldn't care about that. He was completely lost in the sensation of Lark pressing him into the soft, dark leather.

Brody thrilled to the fingers burrowing into his hair. He was pulled impossibly closer, even as his own hands began running freely over the lean, taut lines of Lark's body.

"Much as I love to see you both like this, I think we should move this to the bedroom, guys."

Lark pulled away and stared down at Brody, his eyes unfocused and dazed with lust and a hint of confusion.

"Wolf," Brody managed to gasp, reaching up to run his hands through Lark's blond hair and pulling him in for another quick, passionate kiss before releasing him.

Zak pushed at Lark's hip until finally their small lover groaned and got up to stand beside the couch. The evidence of his desire was clearly outlined by the tight fit of his pants. His lips remained slightly parted and swollen from their enthusiastic kissing.

"Hurry," Lark urged, reaching down to drag Brody up beside him and not even waiting until Zak stood up to start moving them to the bedroom.

As soon as the door closed behind them, Lark started working on the buttons and fastenings of Brody's clothes frantically. Brody—caught up in the mad, feverish need—began tugging and tearing at Lark's, sparing just enough time to look over to make sure Zak was also shedding his shirt and pants.

"Oh! Need you!" Lark moaned, thrusting up against Brody when finally they were both naked. "Need you both."

Brody pushed into Lark, feeling his erection move and rub across Lark's pale, smooth belly. Brody groaned and closed his eyes, desperately fighting for control. It would be so easy to give in and just continue to move and thrust against Lark until they found release. Everything felt so tight and tense inside Brody that he welcomed the sweet oblivion that orgasm promised.

"On the bed, Lark," Zak growled, his voice so low it rumbled through Brody.

Zak pulled the two of them apart and pushed Lark towards their bed. Scurrying to comply, Lark's sweet, rounded ass was the only thing Brody could focus on as the smaller man scrambled across the sheets to lie in the middle of the bed. Brody continued to stare in amazement as Lark reached for the lube, spread his legs and after taking a generous amount, began to work his fingers in and around his own hole.

"I want you, Brody," Zak breathed into his ear from behind him, before gently taking the earlobe in a soft, teasing bite. "I want to sink my cock into your tight hole and fuck you so long and hard. And I want you to be inside Lark while I do it, baby. Want to thrust into you and feel it pushing you into him. Going to fuck you both so good!"

Brody arched back into Zak's furry chest. The way Zak spoke to him. The feel of his solid, warm body and the steel hard cock that pressed into Brody's back. It was almost too much. Then Zak's hand came around and very gently squeezed with just the right amount of pressure for Brody to be able to get himself under control again.

"Not yet, Brody. Soon, baby. Why don't you go help Lark while I get the supplies?"

Brody wanted to turn around and launch himself at the man when he felt Zak pull away—the sudden absence of the firm, warm body riding over his back was almost painful. But the sight of Lark's hole, gradually opening for him right before his eyes, and the knowledge that Zak would be back soon, helped to soothe Brody just enough.

With deliberate movements, Brody stalked up the bed towards Lark, hungrily eyeing the man, his throbbing cock, and his fingers working at his hole.

"Oh, fuck," Lark moaned, "the way you look at me."

Lark closed his eyes and arched into his own fingers and Brody took the opportunity to lean in for a surprise attack. Without warning, where Lark's fingers entered his body, Brody swiped across with the flat of his tongue and thrilled when Lark's moan rose to fill the room with his ecstatic response.

Brody licked again and again, until Lark's fingers gradually lost coordination and power and stilled while he lost himself to the pleasure Brody was giving him. Taking over, Brody began to combine his tongue and his own fingers to push in beside Lark's and open his lover up. He stretched and prepared Lark with gentle, slow insistence.

When cool lube touched his own hole, Brody started. He hadn't heard Zak return with the supplies.

"Shh. Your turn, sweetheart. Just relax," Zak cooed.

Brody was so glad Zak had given him a head start working to prepare Lark, because the longer the man worked on him with those talented fingers, the less effective Brody became with his own inside Lark's hole—a fact that didn't go unnoticed by Lark.

"Please, Zak. Please hurry. I need more. Now," Lark moaned, tossing his head from side to side in desperation.

Brody felt more lube added to his already slick hole.

"Mmm…patience, Lark. We don't want to hurt our Brody."

The way Zak called him theirs sent a fresh wave of mingled lust and love coursing through Brody's over sensitised body.

"I'm ready, Zak. Really. Please." Brody wasn't sure whether it was the strangled, urgent sound of his plea, or the need he felt in Zak as his big, strong hands began to tremble with passion, but he felt the fingers slip away. Brody couldn't hold back a groan at their loss, even though he knew it heralded better things to come.

"Here, Brody. Hurry." Zak handed him a condom and Brody quickly rolled the thin latex down his shaft as he watched Zak do the same out of the corner of his eye.

"Oh, fuck, Brody! Come on. Want you inside me. Now." Lark pulled his knees back and rolled his head from side to side on the pillow, completely wanton and desperate. And Brody knew exactly how he felt.

Without wasting another second, Brody brought his throbbing, hard cock to Lark's pulsing entrance and pushed in. One long, smooth slide had him fully seated inside his lover and they both moaned in delight. Brody found he couldn't wait more than a few seconds before he needed to pull out slightly and push back in.

The feeling of Lark's body opening up around him and taking him in was more overwhelming and euphoric than anything Brody could ever remember experiencing. Something about this moment, this one small slice of time between the three of them, was everything Brody had ever longed for. He felt...home.

Then the tip of Zak's thick shaft nudged insistently against him. Without thought, Brody pulled back a little from Lark and tried to thrust himself down over Zak's shaft. He wanted Zak inside him, and he wasn't about to let the man go slow.

Zak's hands gripped his hips tighter and tried to slow his thrust.

"Oh! Slow down, Brody," Zak panted. "Oh, fuck! Just—"

"No! Now! Inside me." Brody almost didn't recognise the sound of his own voice it was so low and filled with a deep, demanding growl.

Whatever it sounded like to Zak, it was apparently exactly the right thing to say, because Brody felt the long thick invasion of Zak's shaft fill him and drive home until Zak was buried balls-deep. Zak's lunge pushed Brody forward, pressing him into Lark until he was buried to the hilt inside Lark's tight hole.

With the three of them joined as deeply and completely as possible, they shared a moan of mixed joy and torment. The seconds dragged out as they all fought for breath.

Zak was the first to recover. He tentatively pulled back, still holding Brody's hips in a bruising, wonderful grip, then thrust back in. On the next pass, Brody joined him, pulling out of Lark and letting Zak's momentum thrust him back in. Slowly, the dance and play of skin riding over skin, of murmured praise and grunts, of pleasure built until it was a cacophony of sound. A noisy meeting of flesh slapping against flesh.

"Ahhhh!" Brody wailed, no longer able to contain his orgasm. "Gonna—"

He felt the cum explode out of the tip of his cock to fill the condom deep inside Lark's body. Seconds later, Lark's hole spasmed around his sensitive, throbbing cock, dragging another, weaker orgasm from him as Lark shot long, spatters of pearly white sperm over their bellies and chests. That was all it took for Zak to call out his release, and Brody felt the cock in his own ass pumping long, hard jerks inside him.

It was too much. Brody's arms trembled and he could no longer support his own weight. Before he collapsed on top of Lark, Brody managed to ease awkwardly down beside the smaller of his lovers. Unable to move, he didn't even have the energy to raise his head when Zak's warm, solid body wrapped around him.

As Brody drifted off to sleep, finally finding the peace and calm that had eluded him all day, he realised that this was it. This was what he had needed and never thought he would ever have. And no one could take it away now. He wouldn't let them. More importantly, he finally knew Zak and Lark wouldn't let them. They all wanted this and they would all fight for it.

Brody realised he had a home at last. He had somewhere that was more than just nice. It was heaven on earth. He would never have to worry about how he was going to pay for it or if someone was going to steal it from him, because home was Zak and Lark.

Chapter Thirteen

Brody gently stroked back Wolf's wild, tangled fringe and smiled to himself. The boy's soft, even breaths around the thumb in his mouth was so peaceful, it was hard to imagine the little tear-away being anything but angelic.

Man, he loved Wolf. Leaning forward Brody placed a small kiss against his sleeping brother's temple and quietly heaved himself up from beside the bed.

Placing the storybook he had just finished reading on the bedside table, Brody stretched the kinks out of his back. He moaned softly at the tiny pops that went off and eased some of the pressure in his spine. Smiling down at Wolf one last time, he padded silently to the door.

He could never have imagined four days ago, as he waited and worried while his lovers where in the hands of the police, that he would ever feel this good again. But here he was, so happy he could almost burst. Even the knowledge that it was Saturday —

traditionally the busiest night of the week in the restaurant — couldn't burst his bubble.

Nothing had happened in days. No letters. No more threats or incidents with the police. Nothing. It had all just disappeared. And Wolf's birthday was only a month away.

Brody's smile morphed into a true, wild grin of joy. This year, for the first time ever, there was enough money to go all out. There would be presents and cake and balloons. And of course, two very special men to share it all with them.

Carefully opening the door so as not to make a sound, Brody slipped out of the room and sighed in relief. Things were about as perfect as he could ever imagine them being — Wolf was finally down for a nap, there was still over an hour before they had to be down at the restaurant to get things ready, and Zak and Lark were waiting for him in the living room to make the most of it. For the first time in forever, Brody could actually see possibilities, not just problems, opening up before him. Life was good.

But the ecstatic smile slipped from Brody's lips when he heard raised voices drifting down the corridor.

What's that all about?

He'd heard the faint chime of the front doorbell a few minutes ago, but had been enjoying watching Wolf go to sleep too much to be overly bothered with it. They weren't expecting anyone, so he'd ignored it. Most of the time it was either someone wanting to sell something, pontificate, or drop off supplies for the restaurant, anyway, and Zak dealt with those sorts of things.

Whoever they were, if they woke Wolf, Brody was going to be pissed.

Heading purposefully down the long corridor from the bedrooms to the living room to ask them to keep their voices down, Brody slowed when he heard the muffled voice again. The thick walls and distance garbled it, but it sent a shiver of apprehension down his spine. It sounded like —

"You're ruining everything!" Rio suddenly screamed, loud and clear.

"What are you talking about?" Lark's voice sounded tight and high with fear.

Brody crept forward. Something in the way his lover spoke urged him to be very careful and very quiet.

"You and him!" Rio shouted back. "Flaunting your disgusting perversions all over the place!"

"Rio, you're not making any sense. Calm down and let's talk about this," Zak replied in the kind of voice used to placate a madmen as Brody reached the end of the hall.

Stepping into the entrance to the living room, anxious to find out what was going on, Brody froze in shock.

Rio was standing in the middle of the room with a gun trained on Lark and Zak.

The panic that filled Brody at the sight ran parallel to the calm section of his brain that sized up the situation logically and realised he'd been pretty stupid to keep heading in the direction of the yelling. Why did he have to pick this moment to ignore his natural instinct to run when he heard raised voices?

If he had run, he could have made it to the bedroom and called the police. He could have taken the cordless phone and locked himself in Wolf's room and —

Wolf! Oh, God! Wolf! Brody's heart pounded wildly in his chest.

His breath hitched in his throat when Rio glanced over to see him standing frozen in the hallway, gaping like a landed catfish. The chance to run was well and truly gone now.

Rio turned hard, burning eyes on him without shifting the gun away from the centre of Lark's chest. Brody felt a cold sweat break out across his body.

"There you are. I was wondering where the hell you'd got to." Rio motioned with a barely perceptible movement of the gun's barrel. "Please come in and join us."

"Rio, let Brody go." Zak's tone was now hard and cold. "He's got nothing to do with this."

"I don't think so," Rio replied smoothly.

"Rio! What the fuck are you doing?" Brody managed to force out.

Brody could understand the gun. He could even understand the cold, menacing tone of Rio's voice that sounded chillingly rational and sane, but so obviously wasn't. What he couldn't understand was why.

"I'm taking care of things, the only way they can be taken care of, apparently."

"Rio—" Brody started to say, determined to try to reason with the man, even though it probably wouldn't do any good. At least it might buy them some time.

"No!" Rio bellowed. "I'm through trying to do this the easy way. I gave them plenty of opportunity to end it. To walk away and do what's right. It ends now. Even if I have to do it myself. It's people like them that bring all of us down."

"Rio, what are you talking about. Lark and Zak aren't—"

"Don't! Just don't!" Brody could see Rio was getting more and more agitated. The wild look in his eye was truly terrifying now. "It's their sort of sick, fucked up perversions that will send the whole gay rights movement back into the dark ages. We've fought and marched and campaigned for years! Then some stupid fuck-ups like them come along and threaten it all. I'm sick of how many times I've seen it. And it's always the only thing the fucking media ever report! I have no idea how you managed to fool the police, but I'm going to fix the problem once and for all this time!"

"Brody..." Zak cautioned, but Brody ignored him.

"That was you? You called the police?" Brody was clutching at straws, but he knew he had to keep the man talking. He needed to get Rio's attention away from Zak and Lark. And whatever else happened, he couldn't let the gun go off.

"Of course it was me. Get a fucking clue!" Rio's eyes narrowed as he focussed in on Brody. "You know I really can't believe you either. How can you allow that child anywhere near these perverts?"

"Don't talk about them like that!" Brody snapped back, bristling at the way Rio was talking about the men he loved.

"They don't deserve to live!" Rio spat.

"Shut up! You don't know anything about them. They're a hundred times the man you are. You're a fanatic, Rio. Get—"

"Brody!" Lark's voice pleaded with him to back off, but it was too late.

"Shut the fuck up!" Rio bellowed, the gun shifting slightly off target from where it had been aimed directly at Lark's chest.

Spittle was collecting in the corners of Rio's thin mouth as he spoke, making him look even more insane as his anger rose and the wild light in his eyes morphed into rage. Brody really didn't care. In fact, he wanted Rio to get angry with him. Maybe it would save Lark and Zak.

"You're a prejudiced, intolerant, self-righteous jerk, every bit as bad as the people you claim to be trying to fight and march and campaign against."

"Brody!" Zak snapped in warning.

"Don't you fucking talk to me like that!" Rio took a threatening step towards Brody, the gun way off target now.

Brody felt a spike of triumph fused with fear.

"I was fighting for the meagre rights you enjoy now before you were born, you stupid little cock-sucker!"

"You're still an asshole!" Brody retorted, relieved to see the gun waver slightly towards the ground as Rio became more and more distracted.

"You're as bad as they are—!" Rio began to scream.

"Brody?"

Brody's heart leapt up into his throat at the sound of the small, sleepy voice behind him.

Rio started in surprise at the sound of Wolf's voice in the corridor and the gun jerked back up to chest level, moving towards the unexpected noise.

Then everything happened in a blur.

Zak's roar of fury filled the room as he launched himself at Rio. The deafening sound of the gun firing exploded in Brody's ear, but all he could focus on was getting to Wolf.

Spinning around, he ran full tilt back towards his brother.

Wolf's eyes were wide and terrified. He looked too scared even to scream.

Meeting the small boy in the hall before Wolf could make it any further into the living room, Brody scooped him up into his arms and ran back down the hall towards the bedrooms. He heard Zak pounding into Rio and Lark screaming, "Don't kill the bastard! I'm calling the police!"

After that, it all became muffled and faded into the background as Brody slammed the door to the master bedroom and locked the two of them in the en suite.

Wolf sobbed into his neck as Brody settled onto the floor, cradling the little boy close against his chest. Brody tried to make soothing sounds, but his mind was screaming and sobbing right along with Wolf, so he wasn't sure how successful he was.

"Where's Lark?" Wolf howled. "I want Zak!"

"Shh. It's okay. They're right outside."

"Lark! Zak!" Wolf began to call, as if summoning them would instantly bring them in and make them safe. Brody wished it worked like that. He'd be screaming out at the top of his lungs, too.

"Are they going to be all right?" Wolf eventually managed to get out between hysterical, hiccupping sobs several minutes later.

"Yes," Brody said firmly, putting all his belief into that one word. They weren't allowed to be anything but all right. They just weren't allowed.

Brody continued to rock and pat Wolf's back, taking an equal measure of comfort himself—from the gesture, and from the fact that there were no more gun shots.

Everything would be all right. It had to be.

* * * *

After what seemed like days, but was probably only about half an hour, Brody heard a gentle knock at the door.

"Brody? Wolf?" Lark's soft voice called through the door.

"Lark!" Wolf shouted, bounding up and running to let Lark in before Brody could stop him.

"Wolf! Wait—"

But it was already too late. Wolf frantically pulled at the lock until it finally sprung open and he could launch himself at Lark.

Lark bent over and wrapped his arms around the small body attached to his legs.

"It's okay. Everything's fine." Lark looked up and Brody saw the reassurance was every bit as much for him as it was for his little brother.

Following Wolf's lead, Brody rushed forward and threw his arms around Lark. It felt so good to hold his lover after the recent terror. The realisation that he could have so easily lost him made Brody weak at the knees and a fine tremor worked its way over his body. He felt his breath hitch in his chest and mumbled his thanks to whatever higher power was listening and had kept Lark safe.

"Zak...?" Brody croaked into Lark's neck, hoping the man would understand.

"He's fine. The police are taking Rio away, but they have some questions."

Brody's arms tightened around Lark. He probably would always react the same way when police were anywhere near him, but Brody fought to stay calm. There had been far too much panic for one day already.

Lark gave him a squeeze back, letting him know without words that he understood, but that it would be okay.

"Hey, Wolf! Do you remember Officer Denkewitz from the other day?" Lark asked, directing his comment to the top of the little boy's head where Wolf still clung to Lark's legs in a fierce hug. "He's here again. I think he'd like to talk to us some more. Do you think that would be all right?"

"I suppose so," Wolf mumbled without looking up. "But make the bad man go away first."

"It's okay, Wolf. You don't ever have to talk to him. He wasn't being very nice so the police took him away." Lark pushed back Wolf's unruly blond hair and Brody felt his heart flip flop. It was such a sweet, gentle gesture of love and affection—like Wolf was Lark's to care for too.

"He's not allowed any ice cream! Not ever again!" Wolf announced, thrusting out his bottom lip for emphasis.

His little face looked so cross and serious Brody had to smile. That was Wolf—judge, jury and executioner. If only it were that simple.

Shivering, Brody pulled away as a wave of unease raced down his spine. The very thing Zak and Lark had tried to avoid all along was most likely inevitable now. The media were going to have a field day with this.

Brody jumped when he felt Lark's hand caress his cheek.

"It'll be all right, Brody. Promise." Looking into Lark's dark blue, sincere eyes, Brody desperately wanted to believe him. "Come on, guys. Let's go before Zak opens the cookie jar and gives Officer Denkewitz all the double-choccy chip ones while we're not there."

Reaching down, Lark took Wolf's hand and led him away. Looking at the two of them like that—his small, energetic lover holding Wolf's hand and talking reassuring nonsense to distract him from his recent terror—Brody's heart ached in the best possible way—so full of love it was almost too much.

They were all together. He just had to keep reminding himself of that over and over again. As long as that didn't change, everything would be fine.

"Come on, Brody," Lark called over his shoulder, "or Wolf gets your share too."

Despite everything, Brody felt a hesitant smile tug at the corners of his mouth. Everything was going to be fine. It just had to be.

Chapter Fourteen

Brody had tried to stay patient and calm. Really he had. It seemed to take years for the police to run through their endless queries and procedures. But finally, they were all gone and peace had been restored in their home. Or perhaps it would be more accurate to say it was quiet, because Brody felt about as far away from peaceful right now as he could get.

Closer to one in the morning than midnight, Brody was completely drained and exhausted, but he knew there was no way he was going to be able to sleep. Not like this — all tied up in knots and strung out on residual fear. Going over and over what had happened for hours on end with police officers and detectives and goodness only knew who else had left him tight and agitated to the point he couldn't stay still and honestly didn't know what to do with himself.

Turning as he reached the couch, Brody continued to pace restlessly around the living room — too wound up to even think about taking a seat.

"Hey." Brody spun on his heels at the sound of Lark's small, tentative voice behind him. "You all right?"

No!

Running his hand through his hair, Brody desperately tried to keep himself together as he nodded anyway. "Where's Zak?"

"Downstairs, locking up the restaurant for the night." Brody nodded again—his chaotic thoughts making it hard to concentrate and form a more complicated reply.

He hoped Zak would be back soon. He needed to be able to see his lover. To know he was safe.

"Everyone was fantastic while we were tied up with...well, you know," Lark continued.

Yeah, he did. The cops had asked so many questions, his head was still spinning.

Lark cleared his throat. "Yeah, the gang kept it all going smooth as silk down in the restaurant. We'll have to think of a special way to thank them all."

Brody continued to pace. He wasn't sure how Lark could trust anyone after the last few weeks. First Gus, then Rio—

Brody pushed even the name out of his head. If he started to think about Rio again, he'd start to think about the look he'd seen in the other man's eyes as he held a gun on Zak and Lark. Then he'd start to remember that all-consuming terror as the gun had moved towards—

"I need to go check on Wolf."

It had taken the little boy forever to fall asleep tonight. Brody needed to make sure his brother was still all right and sleeping soundly. To make sure he hadn't woken up frightened or...or something.

"Brody, he's fine. I just checked on him. And so did you five minutes ago. Why don't you sit down and—"

"I can't! I just...I keep seeing him here. In our home. With the gun pointed at you and Zak and...and then the cops and—"

"Calm down, Brody. He's gone. They're all gone now. We're fine and everything's going to be okay."

"But you could have died. And Zak too. And Wolf! What if he'd shot Wolf?"

Lark shivered. "Don't! Just...just let me make you some warm milk or something. We can snuggle on the couch while we wait for Zak—"

"I don't want warm milk! I want..." Brody's voice trailed off as he finally stopped and took the time to really look at Lark.

As he studied Lark's face, he could see the composure was actually only a thin mask, and all around the edges, big cracks were starting to form. Lark wasn't anywhere near as okay as he pretended to be. In fact, the thin compression of his bloodless lips, the tight lines around his eyes and the tense way he held himself at the moment suggested he was every bit as upset and traumatised by the day's events as Brody was—maybe even more so.

Lark had been so calm and collected through the afternoon and into the evening. He hadn't let anything phase or shake him as he recounted the story over and over again. He'd help comfort Wolf, supported Zak and soothed Brody whenever the presence of the police became too much. But now he didn't look so good.

Brody suddenly realised Lark must have been one of those people that held it all together during a crisis, then fell apart afterwards. And he wasn't helping his lover right now by pacing around all tense and anxious.

"I'm sorry, Lark." Stepping forward, Brody wrapped Lark up in his arms. And Lark immediately hugged him back—fiercely clutching at him and pressing close.

The sound of the front door opening made Lark jump a little in his arms, and Brody finally started to realise just how upset Lark really was.

"It's me," Zak called out.

"We're in here," Brody replied, still holding Lark tight.

The sound of keys being tossed into the bowl on the hall table was followed by Zak's footsteps in the hallway.

"Are you guys okay?" Zak asked as he entered the living room and hurried across the space towards them.

"I don't think so," Lark confessed against Brody's chest.

In an instant, Zak was at their side. He wrapped his arms around them both in one go and held them close. "I'm so sorry. I promised I'd keep you all safe. I promised I'd protect you and—"

"It's not your fault!" Lark's embrace became almost painfully tight around Brody. "It's not anyone's fault but that bastard Rio's!"

"How could he do something like that?" Brody whispered into the top of Lark's head where it rested under his cheek. "I just...I don't understand."

"I don't think we should try," Zak replied. "Like you said, he's a fanatic. One that finally went off the deep end. I just...I wish I'd seen it sooner. I wish I'd...done more to protect you all."

Lark's answer was to pivot in their embrace and wrap his arms around Zak. Brody joined him—clinging to the bigger man, needing to feel the safety he always found in Zak's arms and to let his lover know without words he still felt it. No way did he blame any of this on Zak. Or Lark. It all rested squarely at Rio's feet.

"Do you think he'll get out on bail?" Brody asked.

"I'm not sure," Zak confessed. "Officer Denkewitz is hopeful they'll be able to hold him. And Mac said he'd do his best to make sure he stays locked up. At least until the trial. After that…"

"I don't want to talk about him anymore," Lark said, burrowing further into Zak's arms.

But Brody couldn't let it rest. "What about the media? What's going to happen when they get hold of this? What are we going to do?"

"We'll deal with that if and when it happens," Zak replied. "Let's not start getting ahead of ourselves and fussing over problems we haven't come across yet."

"But—"

"Enough, Brody," Zak said in a gentle reprimand, pulling him in close until he could seal their lips together.

Within seconds the stress, tension and fear of the day turned the kiss into something wilder—cutting off any further questions, fretting or even thought with the wicked play of their tongues.

He heard Lark whimper, then rise up on his toes to join them in a heated three-way kiss that sent shivers of desire racing through Brody's already over-stimulated body—pushing everything else but the need and longing he'd felt for the two men ever since first setting eyes on them to the back of his mind.

"Bed. Now. Both of you," Zak growled between kisses.

Yes!

Something settled inside Brody at the deep commanding tone of Zak's voice, even as his lust went into overdrive. Yes, this was exactly what he needed — what they all needed. To lose himself in his lovers and know that they were safe and whole. And his.

* * * *

Lark felt breathless and squeezed tight. Stumbling down the hallway together helped. He wanted — no, needed — to be with Zak and Brody. But in truth, nothing felt quite right at the moment.

Normally being short didn't bother him at all. But right now he felt...small. Like everything that had happened and the long afternoon of holding it all together had finally crashed in on him, crushing him down to a fraction of his normal self. He was all off-kilter and...twitchy. Itchy in his own skin.

Finally reaching the bedroom, the door closed and the lock tumbled into place. But Lark still didn't feel safe. He needed to be connected to his lovers — needed them in and on and surrounding him until the whole world was a distant memory and there was just the three of them, lust and love.

Lark's only comfort was that both Zak and Brody seemed to be just as frantic and needy right now. They all urgently pulled and tugged on each other while they kissed and caressed and struggled to strip off clothing. Shirts and pants and underwear fell in random, haphazard patterns around the room until they were all completely naked, still licking and kissing and fondling and working hands over each other's bodies. As if desperate to reassure themselves their lovers were alive and well.

Hands wandered and tweaked and caressed. Lark slid one of his down Zak's hard, hot belly until he could take Zak's thick cock in his hand and begin to massage his lover's shaft. With each stroke he made sure to apply just the right amount of pressure with his thumb to the sensitive spot below the turgid head.

"Oh! Yeah, right... Oh! Right there!"

Zak threw his head back in bliss and Lark groaned right along with him, humping against Zak's thick thigh to relieve some of the ache in his own leaking cock.

"Oh!" Zak cried again, this time in a higher pitch — apparently already on the very edge of orgasm.

Lark instantly stilled his hand. He didn't want Zak coming. Not yet. He needed far more — they all did. More than the quick relief of a hand job.

"Want you. Want you both so much. Need —" Brody moaned, obviously beyond forming coherent sentences now.

Zak panted, eyes closed and muscles tense — as if struggling for control as well. "Bed. Now. Both of you."

While perhaps not terribly articulate, that sounded like the best idea any of them had had all day to Lark. He tugged furiously at them, urging his lovers to get a move on until they all collapsed onto the bed in a tangle of legs, arms, wandering hands and hard, urgent kisses.

"Need you. Can't lose you. Need you both so much." Brody was breathing hard, his voice tight and strained as he reached down to wrap his hand around Lark's cock.

Lark nearly shot right then and there as Brody began to stroke him with a firm, determined motion. Fortunately, Zak swooped in — slowing Brody by joining him in wrapping his hand around Lark's cock.

"Slow down. I want to do this right. To...to take care of you both. Properly."

Reaching across, Zak snagged condoms and lube from the bedside table. Then he kissed softly at Lark's temple. "I love you." Turning his head, he did the same thing to Brody.

And there was nothing else to say. The sweet, gentle caress, the words — they swelled inside him, opening him up again and pushing away the small, scared feeling deep inside. Everything had clamped down to protect him, to keep him safe and moving during the afternoon, but it hadn't let him go after the crisis had passed. But knowing Zak and Brody were alive and loved him — it was everything and the only thing he'd ever needed. He focussed on that and pushed everything else away.

"I love you both so much. Want to feel you both fucking me. Please. Please," Lark begged.

He needed it. Had to feel them and know everything was going to be all right now.

Brody kissed him. "Anything you want, Lark. Anything you need. Love you so much."

Lark scrambled to his knees. In an instant Brody was covering him. Holding him and completely surrounding him with the warmth of his body. He felt more than saw Brody accept lube onto his fingers from Zak then begin to finger and prepare his hole — gently circling and relaxing before pushing in to start loosening tight muscles.

Brody's fingers inside him were magic — so exactly what he needed right now.

"Oh, yeah! Need you, Brody. Need you so much. Do it. Do it now!"

"Patience," Zak said. "I need to get Brody ready first."

Trapped beneath Brody, Lark experienced through his connection to his lover Zak beginning the preparations. He felt Brody push back eagerly as Zak's fingers breached him. He heard the moan against his ear as Zak stretched Brody open. And he felt the fine tremors of need vibrating against his back. Brody's breath stirred the hairs of his nape as he panted — desperate for more.

Finally, Lark couldn't wait.

"Now! Need you now! Brody! Zak! Please!"

Brody shifted his hips into position and Lark pushed back to let the soft, slick pucker of his hole meet the tip of Brody's cock. Yes. This was what he wanted. What he needed.

In fairness, Brody tried to go slow, but Lark's body demanded more. Now. He thrust back hard and took the head of Brody's cock in one sweet moment of agony, then pressed on — not stopping until Brody was buried balls deep inside him.

"Oh, fuck!" Brody cried.

"Wait! I need...I need to be with you," Zak whispered urgently behind them.

Lark held very still as he felt Zak work his way into Brody's body. Shallow thrusts as they moved and joined together behind him sent electric jolts of sensation racing over his skin as Brody's cock head nudged and stimulated his prostate again and again.

"Oh...move. Brody...Zak...somebody. I need..." Lark moaned and thrashed his head from side to side as he clung by his fingertips to control.

"Hush." Zak reached forward and stroked Lark's hip — soothing the reprimand with his warm caress. "You ready, Brody?" Zak asked, ever the protector.

Fortunately, Lark felt Brody nod against his back. He couldn't take any more waiting.

Echo's of the slow thrusts Zak began into Brody moved forward into Lark, gradually building in intensity as Brody started to add to the force. It was perfect — all three of them joined and moving as one. A blissful rhythm that went on and on.

Then Brody's hand reached around Lark's body. All it took was the lightest of touches to his shaft and Lark's straining cock burst into orgasm, pushing long jets of warm cum out of his body and across Brody's hand and the sheets beneath them.

Within seconds, he felt Brody's cock throbbing in his ass. Zak cried out immediately after as the chain reaction of their lovemaking claimed them all.

Finally, after long moments of ecstasy, Brody collapsed on the mattress beside him and Zak followed him down. Carefully avoiding the wet patch, Lark eased himself down too — straight into Brody's waiting arms.

Lark closed his eyes and sighed with a mix of relief and contentment. His lovers had given him exactly what he'd needed — shelter from the storm, a place to come home and centre himself again.

Wiggling and squirming, Lark rolled over until he could press a kiss to Brody's chest.

"Love you." Reaching over he stroked Zak's arm where it rested over Brody and cradled them close. "Love you too."

This was it — all that mattered. The three of them together and safe in each other's arms.

Relaxing against Brody, listening to them all breathing together, Lark let himself drift slowly off to sleep—exhausted but finally feeling a little more like himself again, peaceful and settled.

Epilogue

When the doorbell rang to announce the last of Wolf's friends arriving for the party, Zak didn't even bother looking over to see if Lark or Brody would be going to answer it. Brody was just as stubborn as Lark now, about answering the door. Zak guessed he couldn't blame the man after the recent traumatic events that had invaded their lives.

Actually, now that he thought about it, Zak wasn't at all sorry both men demurred, leaving the job of answering the door to him. Besides, the noise level was getting pretty bad with four juiced-up kids in residence. It was somewhat of a relief to be able to turn tail and run away, even if it was only for a few moments.

At the door, Zak used the newly installed peephole to check out who was on the other side. Honestly, he probably would have opened the door to Rio anyway, before he went apeshit, but it still seemed like a good idea to get one put in. It was something that should have been done years ago when they retrofitted the apartment. When it had been strictly a storage area, it hadn't needed one. Now it did.

Zak peered out and spotted the top of a man's head. The man was bent down as if talking to someone at his knee. He couldn't see the man's face, but the stunning, glossy black hair gave the man away regardless.

Raven was one of the parents they had met since Wolf started preschool the month before. He was a single dad looking after his son, and if Zak had been interested, he probably would have described the man as drop-dead gorgeous.

As it was, however, Zak had more than enough good-looking men to chase after and cause trouble. But window shopping, according to Lark, was still very much allowed, and Zak found he could truly appreciate Raven's fine, masculine form — the sleek muscles, the trim waist, the tight ass covered by tighter black jeans. Yep, Raven was definitely one fine specimen.

Opening the door, Zak smiled down into the huge brown eyes of the miniature copy of Raven that stood clutching his father's hand. "Hello, Ryan. Come in, we're just getting started."

The little, dark-haired boy silently held up a present, very carefully wrapped in homemade wrapping, like it was some sort of toll for admission. Zak smiled gently and stepped back, aware that Ryan might be intimidated by his size. Raven was barely five-six in boots, and Ryan almost looked like a dark pixie, he was so small and slight.

"It's okay. Why don't you go in and give it to Wolf. He's in the living room."

Carefully removing his shoes, Ryan headed down the hall. He'd been over once or twice already to play and knew his way around, but the boy still looked a little cautious and wary.

Much like his father, Zak thought as he looked back to see Raven watching him before the man quickly ducked his head away. Zak found himself wondering what Raven's story was.

"Hi." Raven's voice was almost too soft to hear.

Zak considered the man for a moment. He wondered how Raven ever managed to meet people. He looked so incredibly uncomfortable just saying hello. No wonder Lark had taken him under his wing and invited the man and his son over so often in the last month. Zak had a feeling they'd be seeing a lot of Raven and Ryan in the future.

"It's nice to see you again, Raven." Zak held out his hand to shake and Raven returned the gesture somewhat awkwardly.

"I...umm...I h-heard what happened...last month...with the guy that tried to...I just wanted to say...I'm really glad you're all okay."

Zak was pretty sure it was the most he'd ever heard the man say. Fair enough, he hadn't known Raven terribly long, but he'd probably just doubled the amount of words Zak had ever heard come out of his mouth. And it'd obviously taken him weeks to work up to saying it.

"Thanks. It could have been a lot worse. I'm just glad it didn't seem to have any long-term effect on Wolf."

Raven nodded, lowering his eyes again.

Actually, Zak was even more grateful that the media circus he had expected around the issue had never eventuated. It had been a lucky combination of factors. Firstly, the police tried very hard to downplay the situation. The last thing they wanted was every evangelist and nutter in the country landing on their doorstep and causing trouble. And secondly, the newly elected local mayor – the one who had pledged to 'tackle the depravity attacking the city' – had been caught, on film, coming out of a notorious gay brothel. The media frenzy had rivalled a pack of sharks at a bait ball.

Zak knew it wasn't completely over yet. They all still had to go through Rio's trial, and no one was sure what that would entail. It was still too early. They weren't even sure what Rio was charged with. They knew now from the private investigators that Gus had been responsible for the vandalism – one final fuck you before he had taken off to his sister's – but Rio was behind all the letters, and of course the final attempt on their lives.

Honestly, Zak just wanted to forget all about it. They had a really great crew in the kitchen now. Dave and Andy were still with them and the same as always. Absolutely nothing seemed to faze either man for long.

Dave just gave the world the finger and moved on to the vegetable prep, and Andy would dryly tell it to fuck off and prepare another sauce. And their latest addition, Mark, was working out so well they'd ended up offering him the position as head chef. They could manage for a while until they found a new mains chef again, but Mark was simply too good to risk losing. He ran the tightest kitchen Zak had ever seen. And, bless the man, he'd offered to help out with the food today.

Lark hurried into the hall, his eyes brightening suspiciously when he spotted Raven. Zak wanted to groan in protest. What was the little troublemaker up to now, he wondered.

"Hi, Raven! I'm so glad you came! Would you mind helping Mark in the kitchen for a second? I really think he needs an extra set of hands in there, but Zak and I need to get the games organised before the revellers revolt."

An ear-splitting squeal arose from the living room to punctuate Lark's little speech.

Raven's eyes widened and he headed straight for the kitchen, obviously glad to be hurrying away from the noise. Lucky bastard.

Zak looked over to see Lark watching Raven's tight ass disappear into the kitchen.

"What are you up to?" Zak asked bluntly, crossing his arms over his chest.

Lark peered up at him, eyes wide and innocent and completely unconvincing. "What?" he blinked, unable to hide the smile that tugged at his lips and showed how self-satisfied he was feeling right then.

"Mark no more needs help in a kitchen preparing food for this lot than I need to put on a tutu and start dancing the nutcracker suite."

"Actually, the kids could probably use a little distraction. It might calm them down…"

"Lark!"

Lark got up on his tiptoes and kissed Zak's cheek. "Do you really want to know?" he asked with a cheeky look in his eyes.

Zak considered his lover for a few seconds. Who knew what was going through that devious little mind when he thought to set up a meeting between Mark and Raven. Zak wasn't at all sure he wanted to know after all.

"No," Zak finally agreed.

Just as Lark looked likely to tell him anyway they heard Brody bellow for help in the living room.

"Let's go rescue our lover before the kids tie him up somewhere," Zak suggested, heading off whatever Lark had been about to say.

"Mmm...Yes, I think we should be the only ones allowed to do that," Lark whispered and Zak let a quick burst of laughter slip out.

Yep, great minds really did think alike.

About the Author

Jade Archer was born in 2010 after a prolonged pregnancy and labour of over 34 years! I've decided she is about 24, enjoys long walks in the country because she does not have five kids and a husband to care for, eats as much chocolate as she wants because she never has to worry about putting on weight (must be all those long walks!) and can often be found planning her next whirlwind world tour or endlessly typing away (without any interruptions) on another hot and steamy erotic romance. It might be space pirates; it might be shifters or a lonely vampire with a hunger for the girl next door, one thing is for sure, she loves variety and cannot wait to meet the next characters destined to fall in love.

Jade Archer loves to hear from readers.

You can find her contact information, website details and author profile page at http://www.total-e-bound.com

Total-E-Bound Publishing

www.total-e-bound.com

Take a look at our exciting range of literagasmic™
erotic romance titles and discover pure quality
at Total-E-Bound.